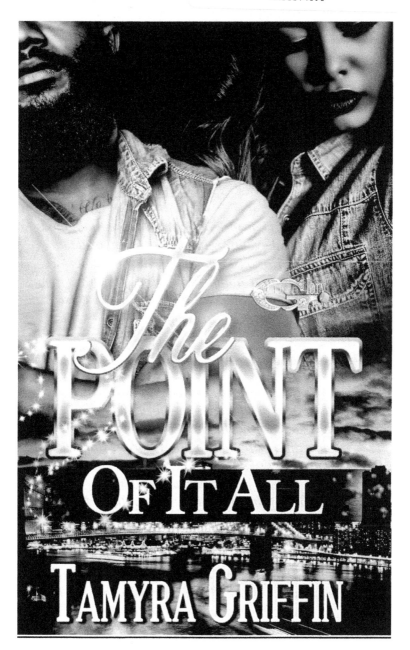

The POINT

OF IT ALL

TAMYRA GRIFFIN

The Point Of It All
-Written By-
Tamyra Griffin

Copyright © 2016 by True Glory Publications
Published by True Glory Publications
Join our Mailing List by texting TrueGlory to
64600 or click here
http://optin.mobiniti.com/V2Yr

Facebook**: Author Tamyra Griffin**

Acknowledgements

First and foremost, I have to think my heavenly father through whom all blessings flow. To my mother, one of my best friends....I thank you. For planting the literary seed which led to my love of reading writing. To my father, I thank you for your love, support and talking to me like I was an adult before I could understand what you were saying. I love you.

I have to give a special shout out to my chicas aka the Golden Girls (Shanay, Lamia and Markeena). Thank you for enduring my "blonde moments" and being my support system. To my lil sis/cousin Leslie.....thank you for being that voice of encouragement when I needed it. I'm still older than you, so don't take it to the head.

To my Flibbitygibbit, thank you for the love and encouraging me to dust off the laptop and continue writing (Even though you wanted to talk when I was in my zone). I still love you though.

I'd have pages of acknowledgments and thank you's if I wanted to thank everyone individually, so I think my entire family for your love and support. Special shout out to my "Bad Assistant" aka Little/Big brother. I also have to give a special shout out to my "Yen" who's played a major part in broadening my outlook on love.

Thank you to the True Glory Publication family and last but not least....Shameek Speight. I can't thank you enough for the opportunity to display my talents, not just as an author but as your editor. Because of you and the opportunity you've afforded not just myself but other aspiring writers, I'm realizing a dream. I honestly can't thank you enough.

This one is for you Gran! Love you always.

Oh, and to my readers…..I hope you enjoy and thank you for your support. Xoxoxo.

Table of Contents

Chapter 1

"Damn! I'm the luckiest mu'fucka alive. It should be illegal to have a wife as sexy as your ass is. Bring all that over here and sit it on Daddy's face."

"Mmmm, you know I love it when you talk dirty to me Daddy." Orchid moaned, crawling across the bed and up her king's body.

"You corny……but I love you to death." D. said, kissing her lips.

"I love you too babe."

"Quit your stalling and get dat ass up here."

"Oh, you think you about to put in some work huh?"

"I know I'm 'bout to put in work. Make that ass tap out."

"Oh, we'll see who'll be tapping out."

Orchid straddled his face as he licked his lips, onto his awaiting tongue. Grabbing two hand fulls of ass, he began sucking gently on her clit.

"Mmmm damn. You wasn't playing." She moaned as she gently rocked as he continued sucking her swollen pearl.

Leaning forward, she stroked his rock hard dick before spitting on it causing him to moan. Licking around his head first, Orchid took him into her warm mouth until she felt the head in her throat. Slowly deep throating his massive organ she moaned as he continued the assault on her clit.

"Shiiiiiit!." She paused to moan she felt his thumb massaging her chocolate star, bringing on her first orgasm.

When he began thrusting his tongue in and out of her opening while playing with her ass, she knew his ass was showing off. After coming down off the high from her first orgasm, she took him back into her mouth. Stroking him as she sucked on the head, she heard his toes cracking. Taking him deeper into her mouth, he stopped tongue fucking her to moan.

"Damn ma! You putting the jaws to this mu'fucka tonight. Fuck!" his moans smothered by her juicy folds pressed against his lips.

"Shut up and eat the pussy."

"Fuck! You turn me on with that shit." He moaned before attaching himself back to her clit.

Feeling her fourth and most powerful orgasm slowly taking over her body, Orchid sat up and began to grind into his fat tongue.

"You 'bout to come again huh?"

"Yeesssssssss!"

"Yes what?"

"Yes Daddy! Damn I love your ass." Orchard moaned as she felt her juices spill from her and her husband catch them all with his tongue.

"Damn you taste good. Assume the position."

"Nah.....i'm not done with you yet." Orchid moaned, leaning forward to take him into her mouth again. Bobbing on his dick with no

hands, D moaned and held onto her ass for dear life as she sucked him dry.

Sitting up looking back at him, she dantily whipped the corners of her lips and blew him a kiss. Crawling down his body, she lowered onto him and began a slow grind. Feeling his strong hands around her waist, she let him guide her rhythm. The volume of her moans heightened when his thrusts hit her spot with precision. Sitting up, he grabbed a hand of her long, silky hair.....kissing and licking on her neck as he thrust into her.

"You love me?"

"Yes, I love you." Orchid moaned.

"Tell me you'll never leave me."

"I'll never leave you daddy."

"Fuckin' right!" he moaned hitting her with the death stroke until his seeds filled her and her limp body lay against his chest.

*****

"Your husband was hit for times. The back....."

Pow!

"The leg......"

Pow!

"And twice in the side."

Pow...pow!

Orchid shot straight up sweating, panting; still clutching a picture of her and the love of her life. Tears streamed down her face at the thought of their last night together, that she was leaving their home and her soul mate was gone.

Kissing the picture one last time, she sat it on the nightstand before covering the bed they shared with a white sheet. Picking up the picture and taking one last look around the bedroom they'd shared for four years, Orchid couldn't help but think about where their roller coaster romance began.

Damonte was her mother's worst nightmare, but he was her dream come true. Despite numerous warnings from her mother, aunts and cousins; as well as her fighting him tooth and nail, he finally wore her down. That was five years ago.

Chapter 2

Orchid hung out with her girls and hot ass cousins, but was always the good girl in the bunch. She went to college, worked, and barely had a sex life. She was also the most attractive out of her clique, which consisted of Saunie, Kiko and her cousin Shelle. When they went out, she gave the brothers no love.....until she met Damonte. He was top dog around the hood her mother repeatedly warned her to stay out of. She was born and raised there and although she was groomed otherwise, the hood was in her.

Any who, she and Shelle were going into the corner store as Damonte was coming out. He locked eyes with Orchid and she gave him her sweetest smile. He returned the favor, climbing into his black and chrome Range that was illegally parked next to the curb.

"Girl, he is fine!" Orchid exclaimed once they were inside.

"Girl!....that's Damonte! He's fine, paid......and I heard that nigga was hung like a horse. He ain't your type though."

"How the hell you gonna tell me what my type is?" Orchid fired back with half an attitude.

"You know what I mean. You need one of those nerdy, college boys that has a rich family with vacation homes and shit. D is straight gutter. Shit, just about every nigga you see around here hustling is under his thumb. Besides.....your mom would have a fit."

"You must want to fuck him, huh?"

"You damn straight!" Shelle laughed. "Hey, but he

ain't smiling at me, is he?"

They left out the store and made their way down the street back to Shelle's house where she lived with her mother, Orchid's aunt Debbie. They made it two blocks and a car pulled up beside them slowly. Not just any car....it was Damonte's.

"Girl, I think he gonna holler." Shell said teasing her long weave.

"Get 'em girl." Orchid said unenthusiastically.

"Yo Shelle, let me holla at you for a minute lady." he yelled and stopped his car.

"I'll be right back." Shelle said gassed up, approaching the truck. "Wsup D....how you doin'?" she said in her best round the way girl voice.

"You know what it is ma. Chillin', tryna make a dollar. How you been?"

"I can't complain....doing the same."

"I heard that. I wanna ask you something.....who's your girl?"

"Oh....that's my cousin Orchid." she replied, low key pissed.

"She not from around the way is she?"

"She used to live around here way back in the day, but she living suburban now. Why, wsup?"

"Just a lil research that's all."

"You want me to bring her over?"

"Nah, a real man never needs a wing man.....or woman in this case. Aiight Shelle, I'll holla."

"Aiight D." she said walking back over to Orchid, cursing under her breath.

"You don't look like the nigga you digging just approached you. What happened?"

"He asked about your ass, that's what happened."

"Are you serious?! What did he say?"

"He just asked who you were and if you were from

around here."

"That's it?"

"That's it bitch. We gotta walk faster, I gotta go to the bathroom." she said annoyed.

Shelle was really feeling some type of way that D wasn't interested in her. But, she couldn't be mad at Orchid. She had nothing to do with his actions. Sensing Shelle was feeling some type of way, Orchid was getting ready to walk out the door when she came out of the bathroom.

"Where you going?"

"Home. I need a shower and you acting all stank." Orchid put her on blast.

"I know….my bad. Hooking up with D would be a major come up for a sistuh."

"Listen at your ass. I'm getting ready to be out. I have a lil more packing to do."

"That's right! You move into your spot next week. We definitely gotta have a house warming."

"We'll do that. I'll call you later."

Her whole drive home all Orchid could think about was D and how fine he was. Shelle was right though, her mom would have a fit, and she wasn't used to dealing with a man of his caliber. She reasoned that he only asked about her and didn't make a move, so he wasn't all that interested……wrong.

The day Orchid had been waiting for and dreading had finally come. She was moving into her brand new home and her mother was moving to Arizona. After dropping off the last of her belongings to her new place, Orchid went back to the home she shared with her mother to say her goodbye's.

"I can't believe you're leaving me." Orchid whined hugging her mother.

"I know…..but this is the opportunity I've been working for." Theresa said referring to her new corporate gig.

"I know. Just know I'm gonna be out there at least once every month or two to bug the hell outta you."

"I'm counting on that. I'm gonna miss this house…….and you."

"Me too mom." she said hugging her mother again.

"Alright, I gotta catch my flight. Don't forget, it'll take a few days for your check to clear……and don't go crazy spending it. You've only been a college graduate for a month and employed less than that." Theresa chuckled.

"Whatever hater." Orchid laughed.

"I love you baby."

"I love you too mom." she said as they walked out their home one last time and got into their cars.

Orchid was sad to see her mom go, but she was ready to start the next chapter of her life. One where her mother wasn't involved in or overseeing every aspect of it.

Theresa was of course a single mom, but instead of depending on the system to take care of her and her two kids, she went out, got a degree, and a job in corporate America. As soon as she made enough money, she moved her family out of the hood and purchased a house. She quickly moved up the ranks at the accounting firm where she was employed and before she knew it, was considered upper middle class. She made sure her kids had everything they wanted and needed but, that wasn't enough to save Byron, Orchid's older brother.

Despite not wanting for anything, Byron started hustling, got busted, and was now in the eight year of his twelve-year sentence. It hurt Theresa to her heart, which is why she'd taken the outlook she had on hustlers and those associated with them......although her ex-husband was a hustler also.

Wasting no time getting her plush new digs in order, Orchid was ready to entertain. One thing her dad did besides staying absent, was make sure that both his kids had anything they needed financially. With the money she'd inherited from her father, the trust her mother had given her and what she was earning as an assistant respiratory therapist, she was able to purchase a modern three-bedroom home not too far from where she'd been living.

Only a week into her crib, Shelle talked her into having a house warming. She insisted it be small, otherwise Shelle would have the whole hood invading her home. So, her guest list consisted of her girls Saunie and Kiko, as well as a few cousins and her two hood fabulous aunts....on her dad's side.

"Girl, this crib is hot! And I have a bedroom for when I wanna stay over." Kiko said excitedly.

"Thank you......and yes you do." Orchid laughed. "Let's go back down before they swear I'm being rude." she said referring to her party guests as Shelle and her aunts were coming up her walkway.

"Heyyyyyy!" her relatives yelled in unison when she opened the door.

"Heyyyy! Thank you for coming." she said hugging her aunts and cousin.

"This house is nice chile. I need a tour." her Aunt Debbie said. "Come on Val." she pulled her sister along.

After giving the tour, they ate, drank, played housewarming games and then opened gifts. Orchid didn't really need anything, but she was very appreciative of the things she'd received.

"Oh, I almost forgot. This is for you too." Shell said pulling an envelope out of her purse.

"What! You got me two gifts?!" Orchid said excitedly.

"Actually no. I just happened to run into D and mention the house warming. He gave me this to give to you when I was leaving." she said handing it to her, looking as she opened it.

"Damn! Can I get some space?" Orchid said laughing.

"Hurry up....damn!" Shell spat.

"Since when you and D get all fly like that?" Shaunie asked.

"We're not. I've never even spoken to him. Shit!" she exclaimed opening the envelope.

"What?! What's wrong?" Kiko asked, the closest to Orchid.

"There's a thousand dollars in here." she said flashing the new Benjamins.

"Get the fuck outta here!" Shelle said becoming salty all over again. "Shit, if I knew that was in there you wouldn't have gotten it."

"Shelle!" her mother exclaimed.

"I was just kidding."

"No you weren't." Orchid said laughing. "I guess I should thank him, huh?" she asked no one in particular.

"Yeah! But how you gonna do that if you haven't

even spoken to him?" Kiko asked.

"There's a card in here with his number on it." Orchid said showing it.

"There you go. So, I say we get cleaned up and go to the club later…..drinks on you." Shelle exclaimed.

"Just scandalous." Kiko said, not really feeling Shelle.

"It's cool. I guess we can do that. You down Kiko…..Saunie?"

"I can't go, I gotta watch my nephew tonight. I'll take you up on drinks tomorrow though." Saunie said.

"It's a date. What about you Kiko?"

"I'm down….but you don't have to buy my drinks. Besides, I'll get the chance to test out my new bedroom."

"Aiight, it's settled. Me, you and lil miss sarcasm are hitting the club."

"Y'all didn't ask if we wanted to go." Aunt Debbie said.

"Mom please, you and Aunt Val ain't going to no club."

"It was a nice thought though." Aunt Debbie laughed. "Let's get cleaned up. Maybe I can make the late bingo."

Orchid was wiggling her way into the denim halter dress she was wearing to the club, when she saw Kiko pulling up into her driveway. She sprayed perfume, grabbed her purse, and went downstairs holding up her dress, to let Kiko in.

"Why are you answering the door with your clothes hanging off?" Kiko laughed.

"Well, rather than having to struggle zipping the back of my dress, I figured my best friend would help a sistuh out."

"Girl.....this is nice. I see you showing off the hips and ass." she said slapping her ass.

"Is it too much?"

"You look good. You make me wanna change."

"Why? You're looking bootylicious as always." Orchid laughed.

"Whatever. I got a half of blunt you wanna hit it?"

"If I mess with that, you gonna have to drive."

"I can do that, but you driving back."

After smoking and having a glass of champagne, they went to pick up Shelle and hit the club. Of course she got in the car talking shit to Kiko, as usual. They went at it like cats and dogs, with Shelle starting every cat fight. She was surprised that Kiko could give as good as she gets, sometimes getting the best of her. Orchid shut this particular bickering match down, wanting to enjoy her high, and the rest of the evening.

They got into the club and there were already wall to wall cuties in the house; and it wasn't even midnight. They found three seats at the bar, ordered their drinks, and turned around to survey the club. Since the dance floor was pretty bare, they kicked it at the bar until the guest DJ showed up and started spinning.....that's when they hit the floor. Of course, Shelle was bumping and grinding on any nigga that looked like they had more than a few dollars, while Kiko and Orchid danced with each other and the occasional busta that approached. The DJ started spinning Luke and they lost it. Kiko and Orchid were freakin' like they were getting paid to do it and all eyes were on them. One pair of eyes in particular that were looking their way was Damonte's. He tossed back the last of his shot, descended the stairs to the dance floor, and made his way through the crowd until Orchids ample, soft body was rubbing against his. He placed his hands on her waist and begin moving with her. When she turned around, she saw it was D and just smiled.

After dancing two songs he leaned over and whispered in her ear, "Can I buy you a drink Ms. Orchid?"

"Maybe I should buy you a drink. Thank you for your gift. I was going to call to thank you, but here you are. I must say, I've never had a man, .let alone one I've never been formally introduced to, give me a G."

"I'm Damonte. Now that we've been formally introduced, how 'bout that drink?"

She nodded, so he took her hand and led her towards VIP. While walking, she text Kiko to let her know where she was….just in case he turned out to be a serial killer. He led her to a plush white booth. After she was seated, he gave the waitress their drink order and sat beside her.

"So….Orchid, huh?"

"Yeah…..my mom's favorite flower. I thought that a lil bit strange."

"It's cool….unique. So, Ms. Orchid…..tell me a lil bit about yourself."

"Nothing much to tell. Just graduated college, working……"

"….And moving. Congrats on the new crib. Maybe I can see it sometime."

"Maybe."

"I like you. Beauty, brains…..and a lil spicy."

"Spicy….that's a way to put it. What about you Mr. Damonte? Not that I haven't already heard a thing or two about you."

"It is what it is ma. I do my thing in the streets, gotta few businesses. I'm trying to do a lil something. Only thing I'm missing is someone to share it with."

"Let's not bullshit each other. You're handsome…..so I know you have one or two or three women you dealing with."

"You got me twisted. I got a couple joins I deal with here and there, but that's not what I want." he said looking into her light brown eyes.

"So….you have any kids?"

"Nah, not a one. I want to be settled before I bring any kids into this world. I'm not trying to deal with no crazy ass baby mama. My mom always told me, "be careful who you have kids with". I follow that shit too."

"Good advice." she said texting.

"Is that your man?" he said smiling.

"No. Actually, I left my girl down stairs and she was asking where I was. I guess I better go." she said getting ready to stand.

"You ain't have your drink yet. Tell her to come up here, my peoples don't bite."

Orchid and Kiko ended up chillin' with D and his crew for about an hour. She found herself becoming more interested in D, forgetting they'd left Shelle downstairs.

"Shit! We left Shelle downstairs." Orchid remembered.

"So!?" Kiko said, feeling one of D's boys.

"She good. She at the bar with my mans." Keon,

D's cousin said.

"She in good hands ma. You want another drink?"
D asked unable to keep his eyes off of Orchid.

"Just one, I'm the driver so I need to be good."

"I got you. So, when can I take you out Orchid?"

"I don't know…when can you?"

"Aiight, aiight……can I take you out?"

"I guess so…..since you did give me such a nice gift."

"If I have my way, there'll be more to come."

It was two weeks before Orchid had the time and energy to go out with D. Part of her hoped he'd lose interest and move on, but the other half was intrigued by the gentleman thug he was turning out to be. Not wanting him to know where she lived, she had him pick her up from Shelle's house. Instead of his Range, he pulled up in a cranberry Lexus with chrome rims and tinted windows. Although she and Shelle were already on her porch, he came up to retrieve his date.

"Damn…..you look good." he said admiring Orchid in the maxi dress she was wearing that showed off all her assets.

"Thank you, you too."

"How you doing Shelle?"

"Coolin'. Make sure you have her home by midnight." she laughed.

"Whatever……and make sure you check on my car too."

"I told you, you just need to leave me the keys."
Shell made a last ditch effort.

"So you can be hanging around with your hood booger ass friends, showing off? Hell naw! The last time you used my car, there were at least five

different weaves that shed all over my seats."
Orchid laughed.

"Whatever hoe. I'll see you later." Shell huffed and went in the house after seeing her plan go up in smoke.

"You got that off." D laughed. "She was hot. So, how'd you get the weave out?"

"I didn't, I traded it in."

"Okay! You got it like that huh?"

"I'm not ballin' outta control or anything. Let's just say I'm good."

"Aiight. Buckle up for safety." he said before peeling out of the parking lot.

Chapter 3

Damonte took her to dinner at an Italian restaurant she'd never even been too. The place was beautiful with its clay walls and plush furniture. Making sure to keep this place in her mental rolodex, Orchid give him a brownie point for his choice. She wasn't expecting the corner pizzeria but he did surprise her.

"Impressed, huh?"

"Let's just say you get a brownie point." she laughed.

"I'll take that. So, what do you do Ms. Orchid?"

"I might smack a person that keeps calling me Ms. Orchid but I'm a respiratory therapist professionally."

"So you in the medical field."

"Yeah, I can't stand the sight of blood, so I needed something in the field that was going to avoid it all together. You should see some of my patients. You don't smoke cigarettes do you?"

"Nah….just bud."

"Good, I thought I was gonna have to pray for you. I still might have to." she chuckled.

She enjoyed the conversation they had over dinner. Instead of the hard, cold killer others made him out to be, she got an intelligent, gentle flirt with a sense of humor. At one point at dinner, she couldn't stop smiling at him.

"What?" he asked, noticing.

"What?"

"You're just staring at me smiling."

"I was just thinking how refreshing you were."

"Aiight, you need to give me more."

"I've never been out with a thug." she made air quotes. "Add the personification of a so-called thug with things I hear and you get a date disaster."

Her statement caused him to burst out laughing. He laughed so hard he had tears coming from his eyes. She had to laugh too.

"Girl, you sure do have a way with words. I like that." he said chuckling more. "I'm glad I could silence the critics."

"The nights not over yet."

Instead of taking her back to her car which was the plan, they took a short drive to a sports bar one of D's peoples owned. They sat in a booth talking and eventually holding hands; then sharing a kiss.

"I'm digging you Ms. Orchid."

She raised her hand to slap him.

"Aiight aiight! I am feeling you though. You got a nice vibe going for you."

"You're not so bad either." she said and smiled.

"I guess I can take that......for now. You ready to roll?"

"I guess I better. I have a half hour drive from Shelle's."

"You can chill at my crib for the night."

"I like you, but you ain't getting no pussy tonight." she said causing him to spit his drink and laugh.

"That's the second time you had me waste good liquor tonight. You wild girl." he laughed some more. "Orchid, to be perfectly honest I can get pussy anywhere. I have a guest room you could sleep in. I just was trying to save you a ride, that's it. Now, if you want to......"

"Don't even think about it. It is kinda late. I need to

get my car though."

"We'll go get it and you can follow me to my crib."

Again another shock, Damonte's house was beautiful. She assumed he had an interior decorator come in, everything was in it's perfect place. He gave her the tour of the house and then a t-shirt to sleep in before leaving her to shower and change. When she came downstairs, he was sitting on the couch rolling a blunt wearing a wife beater and basketball shorts; looking at a game. She felt her yoni twitch at the sight of his tight, muscular, chocolate body.

"What you watching?" she said coming into the living room in the over-sized shirt he'd given her to wear, sitting next to him.

"A re-run of the Boston game. You look cute."

"Thank you. Boston huh? You know that's my squad right?"

"Let me find out you on my team. Okay!"

"Yeah, I love basketball but Boston..........I watch every game. I keep saying I have to make it to a game and never do. Gotta put that on my to do list soon."

"You should go. I try to make a least three a year. Maybe I'll take you."

"That's sweet, but you don't have to. You probably wanna go with your boys, drink beer, burp, and look at ass." she laughed.

"I can look at your ass and drink beer. I guess I can keep the burping to a minimum." he laughed. "You definitely keep me laughing."

"I make it do what it do. So, you sharing your marijuana with me?"

"You smoke?"

"Not really. I take a pull or two every now and

again but that's it. You never know when they want you to pee in a cup."

"I hear that. I guess I can share."

By the time the game was over, she'd smoked half a blunt with D, had her legs in his lap and couldn't stop laughing. D was really feeling her. She was a lil prissy, not really stuck up but he could also see the hood deep in her. He knew that she was just what he needed.

It was two in the morning and they'd both dozed off. Orchid was laying on a pillow in D's lap and his head had dropped backward. D shifted his leg causing Orchid to wake up.

"I am so sorry. I fell asleep on you." she sat up yawning.

"I think we fell asleep on each other." he said looking at her. "You're beautiful even when you just wake up."

"Thank you." she said leaning into him, welcoming the arm he placed around her. "I guess you're a lil beautiful too." she giggled.

"Don't forget sexy."

"I guess you can get that." she said looking up at him, being greeted by his lips.

He pecked her lips softly, not wanting to move too fast and drive her away, but she surprised him by giving him a lil tongue. D wanted her damn bad, but he let her take the lead and had to be satisfied with touching her soft body; copping a squeeze when he could, until she broke the kiss.

"Thank you again for tonight Damonte. I had a good time."

"You're welcome." he said, wanting to kiss her sexy lips again.

"I better go up, I need to leave pretty early." she said standing. "I don't have to worry about waking up to any crazed women standing over me, do I?"

"Still with the jokes. Nah, you good. I don't bring women here."

"Are you calling me a man?" she asked pretending to be offended.

"No, girl……you almost got me. You're here because I think you're special." he said getting up and pulling her close.

"Well thank you." she said and kissed him softly.

"Good night D." she smiled and went up the stairs. Needless to say they both went to sleep with blue balls.

After the wonderful night she'd had, Orchid figured the least she could do was make D breakfast before she left. After preparing French toast, sausage and fresh squeezed orange juice, she placed everything on a tray she'd found and carried it upstairs. She knocked lightly on D's bedroom door.

"Come in." he said groggily.

"Good morning." she almost sang approaching his bed with the tray.

"Word! I get breakfast in bed?" he smiled.

"I figured it was the least I could do."

"Thank you." he said pulling her to him for a kiss.

"Ewww….morning breath." she joked.

"Awwww! It's like that?"

"I'm just kidding, I held my breath." she laughed.

"I'm getting ready to go. I just didn't wanna slip out."

"What you doing today?" he asked before putting a forkful of food into his mouth.

"Besides cleaning my house, nothing until I meet a

friend for drinks later."

"Your man?"

"I don't have one of those. It's a female if you must know."

"Can I see you again....maybe after you get done with your girl?"

"We'll see. I'll call you." she said walking towards his bedroom door.

"You better." he said smiling at her. "You better."

After finishing his breakfast, D got dressed and hit the streets. "Another day, another dollar." he said walking out the door. He called up Keon to let him know he was on his way to him and couldn't get off the phone without answering questions.

"So, what happened with that sexy ass jawn you went out with?"

"Orchid cool as hell. She different from these other bitches out here."

"She must've put it on your ass huh!"

"Nah, I ain't even on it like that. I'm trying to feel her out, see if she wifey material."

"Wsup with her girl?"

"You ain't get the number?"

"Nah. She was cool but she didn't give up the math. Have your peoples hook that up."

"I'll see what I can do. I see you in a minute."

Chapter 4

Orchid couldn't stop smiling all day. She turned up the music, cleaned the house, and showered before laying on her bed wrapped in a towel. Not wanting to spend the night alone in the house, she called Shaunie to see if they were still on for drinks.

"What it do boo?!" Orchid asked when she answered.

"I can't call it. What up with you?"

"Just chillin'. We still on for later?"

"I can't. I forgot my aunts' fiftieth birthday party is tonight. So, that's where I'll be if I value my hearing."

"I heard that. I guess I'll give you a rain check."

"My bad. How'd your date go last night?"

"I had a good time."

"Did you give it up? You know you need to….clear out some of them cob webs."

"Fuck you and no, I didn't. I stayed at his house but we slept in different rooms."

"You's a bad bitch. Every bitch all up and down this county, maybe even the state wanna fuck D and you slept in different rooms?! You need Jesus."

"Whatever." she chuckled. "Call me when you get back from your uh….party."

"If you were a real friend you'll come with me."

"Maybe. I'll hit you back."

"Great." she said aloud.

Since it looked like she was in for the night, Orchid threw on some clothes to run out to the grocery and liquor stores. She hated food shopping so she waited until the very last minute to go. On her way out the door, her cell sang Kiko's ring tone.

"Hey girl!" she answered.

"What up! How'd it go last night?"

"Well. We had a nice dinner, some drinks, then we went back to his house."

"You slept with him?!" Kiko screamed.

"No bitch. It was late so I stayed in his guest room and came home this morning."

"Oh....I was about to give you a high five through the phone. You and Saunie still going out?"

"No, she got something else going on. So, I'm riding solo tonight."

"You going to the club alone?"

"Nah, I'm just chilling in. I'm on my way to the grocery and liquor store to get my supplies."

"You act like I'm chopped liver."

"My bad, I didn't think you wanted to go out two nights in a row."

"I'm not really feeling the club, but we can do a girls night in."

"Sounds like a plan."

"How long you gonna be at the store? Better yet, let me get my shit together and I'll go to the store with you."

"Aiight, I'll wait. Hurry up too."

"I got you."

Once Kiko arrived, they got in Orchid's truck and headed towards the city. They did her food shopping and grabbed a few extra things for the night. After a stop at the liquor store and the red box, they went back to the house.

They talked shit, drank, and smoked a lil bud while Orchid prepared chicken breasts stuffed with spinach and mozzarella, rice pilaf, a garden salad and crescent rolls. They made their plates, put in a movie and took their places on the couch. They were stuffing their faces and hollering at the TV when Orchids cell rang.

"Did you brush your teeth today?" D asked smiling through the phone.

"Yes, did you?"

"Yes. What you doin' beautiful?"

"Chillin'…..stuffing my face."

"With?"

"Stuffed chicken breast, salad, rolls…..with an alcoholic chaser."

"That's right, you out with your girl."

"Actually, she stood me up. So, I'm chillin in the house with my bff."

"Bff….ya'll women boy. So, I guess that means I can't take you out."

"Can I get a rain check?"

"Yeah. Oh, my man wanna know what up with your girl."

"Your man who?"

"Keon, the one that sat with us in the club."

"Oh, what he wanna know?" she asked and waited while his boy talked in the background.

"He said…."

"Matter of fact, hold on." she said dropping the phone. "It's D, his boy wanna know wsup."

"Oh! Girl, I was tripping last night and forgot to give him my number. He was cute."

"Well here, talk to him." she shoved her the phone.

"Hello." Kiko sang into the phone.

"What she say?" D asked.

"Who?"

"Your girl."

"This is her girl."

"Oh, my bad. Hold on."

Orchid watched the movie and ate while her girl giggled and flirted with D's cousin on the phone. She'd gotten into to the movie so she didn't notice Kiko off the phone, staring at her smiling….at first.

"What?" she said not looking at her, but knowing her too well.

"You wanna go out?" she asked still smiling.

"No."

"I knew you'd say that."

"Then why ask?"

"You feel like company?"

"What?" Orchid asked now looking at her.

"I'm trying to chill with Keon and D wants to chill with you. Sooooo…….I figured they could come chill for a minute."

"I wasn't really trying to let him know where I live just yet."

"O…..really. Ya'll been kicking it on the phone for a minute. I'm quite sure if he wanted to kill you he'd have done it by now."

"You so stupid." Orchid laughed. "Fine….but if I end up sleeping with him, I'm gonna fuck you up."

"Bitch please. You'll be thanking me.'

An hour later Orchid stood in the door smiling at D as he and Keon walked up. He got to the door and kissed Orchid before he did anything else.

"Hey ma."

"Hey. I'm glad you decided to stop calling me Ms. Orchid."

"I didn't want you trying to Ike me again." he laughed. "You remember Keon?"

"Yeah, how you doing?"

"Good and you? This crib is tight."

"Thank you. We're in here." she said locking the

door and leading the way to the living room.

"Kiko....your peoples is here."

"Her peoples huh?" D said hugging her from behind. "We brought some drinks......and I got a lil bud." he whispered in her ear.

They talked shit and played cards until midnight. Keon was actually kinda cool and her girl seemed to be really feeling him. Having a lil bit too much too drink and being more comfortable with D, they were laid up in her chaise lounge, with him whispering slick shit in her ear. She damn sure was digging him. They were booed up loving when Keon came over.

"Can I holla at you for a minute dog? Your girl want you too." Keon said.

"Thanks." Orchid said getting up and sitting on the couch sitting next to Kiko. "What you want now?"

"Some dick."

"Are you serious?"

"Yeah ,but not tonight. I just wanna chill. Is it cool?"

"Lucky for you, if he had plans on possibly staying........D was getting some."

"Awwww....get it girl!" Kiko said loudly attempting to give her a high five.

"What ya'll over here all giddy about?" D said approaching Orchid. "Ma, can I holla at you?"

"Yeah, you can help me carry these dishes in the kitchen."

"Damn, she putting you to work." Keon laughed.

"Shut up and take notes. Maybe you can get and keep a girl." D shot back and laughed.

"Ya'll act just like us. So, wsup?" she asked and hopped on the counter swinging her legs.

"You know I'm feeling you.....right?" D said

stepping between her legs and wrapping his arms around her.

"I guess I'm feeling you a lil bit too. So, I guess you think you getting some pussy now, huh?"

"Shit!" he laughed. "That mouth of yours……..is beautiful." he said and kissed her.

"You real nice with it, I will give you that."

"I'm not trying to run game…...it's how I feel."

"You wanna know how I feel?"

"Do tell."

"I feel like……I wanna be with you tonight." she said looking into his hazel eyes.

"Ma, you gonna wanna be with me every night after tonight. Look, I gotta go handle some business, but I wanna come back…...if you'll have a nigga."

"How long?"

"I can be back in an hour. That way I can drop Keon if your girl don't wanna chill."

"I think she wants to. Look, as long as it's an hour I'll wait for you. Unless I have something to keep me occupied, I'll be sleep."

"I know what I have waiting for me when I get back. It may be less than that."

"Alright, I'll wait for you."

She walked her guests to the door and locked it behind them. She wanted to jump and scream at the thought of being wrapped in his strong arms and him invading her walls. She was wet and zoned out thinking of the possibilities.

"Here you go with that dreamy bullshit. I gather he's coming back."

"They're coming back as if you didn't know. Let's go up and get your room set up. You taking the one at the end of the hall. I don't want to hear anything that may give me a mental image." Orchid laughed.

"Bitch, like you ain't gonna be in there with your ass in the air.....hopefully moaning."

Just as he said, D was calling from out front less than an hour later. She had just gotten out the shower so she asked Kiko to let them in and lock up. D walked into her bedroom just as she was sliding her night gown over her plump ass. Instead of being startled she turned towards him and smiled sweetly.

"Hey." she said softly.

"I told you I'd be back early."

"You did." she said climbing onto the bed, grabbing the remote and sitting back. "Make yourself comfortable."

"You wanna drink?"

"A small one."

"You wanna smoke?"

"A lil bit."

"Can I make love to you?"

"Make love?"

"I'm gonna do things to your body that will make you feel so good, saying we're having sex would be an understatement." he said handing her, her drink.

"Sounds promising."

"Oh, you gonna find out."

They talked while they drank and Orchid had taken just a few hits of the powerful weed and was chinky eyed and horny. She scooted down on her pillow until she was on her back, hard nipples imprinting the silk she was wearing. D passed his lips across them slowly, causing her to tingle.

"Come here." she said reaching her hand towards him. She pulled him until they were face to face. "I like you." she said barely above a whisper.

"I like you too."

D began kissing her while she began pulling off what clothes she could until he was naked. He then pulled the thin piece of silk over her head exposing her naked body. "You're beautiful."

"Thank you."

Without another word, he began sucking on her full nipples while she moaned. Figuring her for a good girl, he continued further down and slowly ran his tongue across her clit, causing her to gasp. He smiled mischievously and began sucking her pearl. Orchid arched her back and moaned as he flicked her clit with the tip of his tongue, trying to grab a pillow to muffle her moans, but he took it from her. "I wanna hear you moan." he said and inserted his finger in her to tickle her g-spot while making figure eights around her clit until her legs began shaking and she was moaning his name. "Come on ma......come for me." he said and sucked on her clit until he felt her juices oozing down his hand. He licked his fingers as he stroked his dick. After sliding on the Magnum, he pulled her towards him and spread her legs.

D entered her slowly, wanting to explore every inch of her walls and was welcomed by the tightness of her pussy. He moaned with every inch he entered her until he'd filled her up. He began stroking her slow until she caught his rhythm. Once she did, it was on. He struggled with each stroke as her pussy suctioned onto him, biting his bottom lip trying to think about something else besides how good Orchid felt. Having to stop to keep from coming, she turned the tables on him. She slowly slid down his dick and began working him slowly. He played with her clit as she continued his slow torture.....until she picked up the pace. D began moaning her name loudly, not able to keep it in. He sucked on a nipple thinking it would help, but in a matter of minutes his toes were twitching and he held onto her as he came. Not wanting to let go, he fell back with his arms still wrapped around her.

"That was good." Orchid moaned kissing his neck.

"That shit was great. Ma, you.....never mind." he said enjoying the feel of her lips on his neck.

"You got another condom?"

"Unh huh..." he moaned.

Orchid retrieved the condom and took the old one off. She slid the condom on and began stroking his eleven inches. She watched as he closed his eyes and moaned before mounting him again. She began working him faster....and faster.

"Fuck Orchid!" he moaned loudly.

"What's....my name?" she asked clinching her muscles on his dick.

"Or....Orchid! Shit!" he yelled as she bounced up and down on his dick. He grabbed her ass and thrust towards her, hitting her spot until she was moaning his name, and cumming. Since she was spent, he turned her over and worked her from the back causing her to come quickly and unfortunately him too.

"You know.....that's my pussy now." he said looking into her eyes.

"Actually, it's mine but you can lease with an option to buy."

"Well, consider this a down payment." he said ready for round three.

Chapter 5

After the night D spent with Orchid, he was sprung. He had no desire for other pussy, all he wanted was Orchid. He would be handling business, need a fix, and would drive to her house. They hadn't put a title on their relationship, but he wasn't fucking with anyone else, nor was she and he let niggas know it would be nothing nice if a nigga even thought about stepping to her.

They'd been intimate for a month before D decided it was time to put his stamp on Orchid. He knew she was a hustlas' dream and he didn't want to lose her on some bullshit. It was Orchid's birthday and D wanted to do something other than a party. He also wanted to make their thing official.

"Hey birthday girl!" he yelled into the phone.

"Hey, what's good with you playa?" she said laughing.

"I done told you, I retired. Besides, you gotta nigga all pussy whipped. I ain't going nowhere."

"Are you gonna tell me where we're going?"

"Nah, just be ready in a half. I'm on my way."

"See you in a lil bit."

D was ringing the bell exactly a half hour later with a beautiful arrangement of flowers. "Happy birthday ma." he said and kissed her.

"Thank you. These are beautiful."

"Just like you. So, you ready to roll?"

"Yeah. Let's roll."

D kept her talking while he drove to her destination. It worked until they got close that it was obvious where there were going.

"D…..that's Madison Square Garden?!" she said excitedly.

"Yeah, nice ain't it?" he said grinning.

"Are you…..D?"

"That's right. Game 2, third row seats ma. Happy Birthday."

"Oh my…God. D…..I couldn't ask for a better gift. Thank you."

"You're welcome. You ready for this?"

"Am I."

During the game Orchid was rowdier and louder than D was. She even let out a few burps for good measure, so he was comfortable. After the game she was able to meet and take pictures with KG and Paul Pierce, which really made her day. After grabbing a quick bite, they went back to her house for his favorite part of the evening.

"Ma, I need to handle something right quick. I'll be back in less than an hour."

"D…are you serious?"

"I promise I'll be right back. I still have something to give you."

"Oh yeah……what's that?" she said kissing him and reaching into his pants, stroking his dick.

"Oh…..you gonna get that too, but nah. "

Although she was feeling some type of way, she kissed him and went in the house. She lit some candles, showered and put on a t-shirt to relax in, not knowing how long he would take.

She was lying on the bed watching the high lights of the game hoping to catch a glimpse of herself when D called to say he'd be there in ten minutes. She hopped up, changed out of her t-shirt and into some lace which she knew wasn't gonna stay on long, and D's favorite pair of stilettos. Just as she was finishing, he was ringing the doorbell. She opened the door and stood there for him to get an eye full.

"Damn ma." he said moving close to her and kissing her. "Climb on." he said grabbing her ass as she wrapped her legs around his waist. "I'm getting ready to make this pussy talk in tongues." he said climbing the stairs with her attached to him.

He laid her on the bed and climbed on top of her parting her lips with his tongue and kissing her. He broke the kiss and just stared into her eyes.

"What?" she said smiling.

"You know you're all I need, right?"

"Really?" she said with a half -smile, half smirk.

"Do you know how long I've waited for someone like you?"

"No….tell me."

"My whole life. Ma…..I want to be with you. Not just on some friends with benefits type shit. I wanna make our shit official."

"D……I'm feeling you too but….."

"If you feeling me, what's the problem? You not giving my pussy away are you?"

"D……I'm not sleeping with anyone but you and haven't for a long time. What about you and your uh…..loose ends."

"You must've thought I was playing when I said I didn't want anyone else. Why, when I have the whole fucking package with you? I won't hurt you ma. All I wanna do is take care of you, keep you safe….warm……love you. Give us a chance ma, be my lady."

She looked into his eyes and saw sincerity, so she decided to take a chance. "Alright D….I'll take that chance."

"Say you'll be mine."

"I'm yours……. and you're mine."

"Fucking right." he said and kissed her. "Hold on one second." he said getting up and going into his bag. "Sit up." he said and placed a platinum and diamond necklace on her. "Diamonds for my diamond in the rough."

"D! It's beautiful…..thank you for a beautiful birthday."

"You can thank me by continuing to be you."

She pushed him onto the bed, straddled him, and parted his lips with her tongue before allowing her tongue to dance with his. She broke the kiss and began undressing him and then herself before she climbed back on sliding up until her pussy stared him in the face. He licked his lips and smiled, ready to put in work until she flipped over and began licking the head of his penis.

"Shit!" he moaned, both because of the tingle he felt in his balls, but also because she'd never given him head.

Once she was able to fit his girth into her mouth, she was able to get down to business. He moaned as her warm mouth moved slowly up and down his dick. Finally able to compose himself, he leaned forward and began lapping at her clit and tickling her spot with his finger. He was about to lose it when she started coming, moaning, and sucking on his dick like her life depended on it. His toes twitched and after she'd came all over his face, he couldn't hold out any longer. He palmed her ass, jerking and moaning as she sucked him dry.

Another shocker was that she actually swallowed.

"Ma……you swallowed?' he asked with kid-like grin on his face.

She looked over her shoulder at him, smiled and said, "You my man right….and this is my dick and mines alone…..right?"

"Abso fucking lutely."

"Okay then. Where it at?" she said referring to a condom. She slid the condom on to his dick with her mouth and led it to her opening, sliding him in slowly, her back still facing him. She leaned forward and began working the dick like a pro. "Damn......ma! You....doin' it.....like that! Fuck!" he said holding onto her ass for dear life. He moaned and finally was able to move with her body hoping the sweet torture would last all night.

Since they didn't go to bed until the sun was up, Orchid had no choice but to sleep in. Thinking last night was a dream, she woke up panicked when she smelt food. She was just easing out the bed to put a robe on and investigate when D walked in with a breakfast tray smiling.

"Hey you."

"Good morning." she sang.

"Get back in the bed, it's my turn. Where were you going?"

"I thought there was a hungry burglar in my house." she said laughing at herself.

"You forgot I was here? Damn!"

"Nah baby.....I thought it was a dream. A wonderful dream."

"I'm the real thing ma and I ain't going nowhere. Come on and eat." he said setting up her tray.

"Thank you baby."

"You're welcome. So, what you got planned for today?"

"I was gonna just lie around the house and recuperate. I think you made my uterus shift a lil bit." she laughed.

"You wild. You can rest in the car."

"Where you think you taking me?" she said feeding

him a forkful of eggs.

"I wanna take my baby shopping. I figured we could hit Atlantic City, do some shopping, gambling......stay in a suite. I just wanna be with you."

"Are you sure Keon won't mind?"

"I already talked to him. Besides, Kiko got that nigga occupied. So, is that a yes?"

"It's a yes."

"Aiight. I'm gonna shower and get dressed while you finish up and then we can be out."

"Uh, D.....you forgetting something."

"What?"

"I want desert after breakfast." she said eyeing him seductively.

"Damn, I'm a lucky nigga"

They spent all day going from store to store racking up purchases. Orchid had died and gone to heaven. She almost couldn't see D by the time they were almost done.

"Ma, I'm glad you enjoying yourself, getting your shop on....but my muscles are 'bout ready to call it quits."

"Awww, my poor baby. Let's go back to the room, get you a hot shower and I'll take care of the rest."

"I'm loving this already."

"What's that?"

"Having the woman of my dreams by my side."

Orchid and D were a month into their relationship and everything was smooth as a baby's ass. Orchid even introduced him to her mom when she came to visit and he'd won miss "anti-thug crusader" over. D, was the happiest anyone had ever seen him and he owed it all to Orchid.

Chapter 6

Having one last end of summer cook out, Orchid dressed for a day in the hood and headed out to her Aunt Debbie's house for Shell's end of summer cook out. Shell wouldn't stop talking about all the hood superstars that were gonna be in attendance at the block party. Orchid bounced down the stairs dressed in Capri's, Coach sneakers and tank top ready to get her party on. Although Shell and Kiko weren't cool, she was accompanying Orchid so she'd have someone to chill with when Shelle's merry band of sack chasing, hood boogers got on her nerves. D was already out taking care of business, so it was she and Kiko.

"I'm glad I smoked cause I know your cousin is gonna show her ass."

"You know she is. Thanks for coming with me K."

"You lucky you're my bff and my dick is gonna be here. Otherwise, I'd stay my ass at home."

"I owe you." she said pushing her friend as they walked toward Shelle and the grouping of multi colored hair that surrounded her. "What's buzzin' cousin?" Orchid perked.

"Heyyyy! You made it." Shell hugged her cousin. "Oh....you too. Hey Kiko."

"Hey Shell." Kiko said nonchalantly and took a seat.

"For those of you that don't know, this is my cousin Orchid." she began introducing Orchid.

Orchid and Kiko sat around with Shell and her crew, occasionally stopping to speak to a few old friends and familiars.

The day was going smooth until the biggest sack chaser around the way came switching over towards their table. All the hustlers who knew what she was about and didn't mind peeling off a lil pamper money, were eyeing her in her outfit that looked like it belonged to one of her small children. "Hey ya'll! What we drinking' on?" she said dusting off the bench and sitting.

"A lil wine, just coolin'"

"Wine? Oh, I see. You bring some sophisticates in the hood and you wanna change up." she said looking at Orchid and Kiko.

"Shanell, that's Kiko and this is my cousin Orchid."

"Oh okay. Wait....you the Orchid that's supposed to be messing with D, huh?" she asked swinging her eighteen inch synthetic weave behind her back with four inch, neon nails.

"I'm that Orchid....but I'm not messing with Damonte. He's my man."

"Well....I guess you must be takin' his cell or something 'cause he loves him some Shanell and always came when I called."

"Listen.....Shanell was it? Whatever happened between you and D is in the past and doesn't concern me. As far I go....I'm the present and the future and I don't need to take his cell. He has everything he needs at home."

"Oh shit!" Shell laughed.

"Oh, you one of those siddity hoes with some lip. Well, I'mma show you what a hood ass whipping be like."

"I'm not gonna be out here fighting like a common hood booger." she said looking her up and down. "But don't get shit twisted. You touch me and I'll have to dust this field with your raggedy ass weave."

"That's it bitch!" Shanell yelled taking off her

earrings.

"Yo…..Yo D! It's looks like it's about to go down over there." Keon said.

"I don't give a shit about them hoes." he said texting Orchid.

"Yo, Orchid and Shanell about to throw down." Keon said running over with D on his heels.

"What bitch!? Let me hear some of that mouth now." Shanell shouted as she got in Orchid's face.

"Wow!" Orchid said twisting up her face. "Could you give me a little space?"

"It's on!" Shanell said swinging at Orchid who dodged the punch.

Shanell swung again scratching her face which pissed Orchid off. She dodged another wild swing and landed a right of her own on Shanell's chin, sending her down on her ass. Shell and everyone else watching was cracking up and some cheering.

"The next time you wanna get up in somebody's shit, you better know who you fucking with bitch!" Orchid spat.

"Ma….you alright?" D said running over to Orchid.

"I'm fine daddy. Who is this bitch?" Shanell said getting up, further playing herself.

"I wasn't talking to you hoe."

"I think you better ask Ms. Thang that question. I guess your taste in women was flawed before you met me, so I'm gonna let this one slide." she said shoulder checking Shanell as she and D walked past.

"Damn ma! I'mma have to start calling you the one hitta quitta. What happened?"

"I guess the words out. One of your hoes decided to step to me about interfering."

"Are you serious?! K…..you hear this shit."

"I hear it dog. What up Orchid?"

"Hey Keon. Kiko, I'm not trying to be here too much longer, I'm not really feeling this."

"We can go now if you want." Kiko said getting up and walking over.

"Where you going with your fine ass?" Keon asked chasing behind Kiko.

"I apologize about that ma."

"There's no need for you to apologize. As long as she stays in the past, we good."

"Past? That right there is ancient history. Can your man come over later?"

"He better." she said kissing D.

"I'm gonna chill around here for a minute, what you getting into?"

"I'm gonna talk it over with Kiko and I'll hit you."

After they'd already decided on a girls' night in, Kiko got a call from Keon asking to chill. Being that she's sprung, she said yes and had Orchid drop her off. Riding solo, Orchid stopped off for a movie and a bottle of wine before going home, showering and pitching camp in the living room. She was dosing off when her bell rang, startling her. She recognized D's body and opened the door with a smile.

"Now this really confirms my suspicion of you sabotaging my evening with Kiko."

"I wanted you all to myself. Is that aiight with you?" he said pulling her close and kissing her.

"That's all you had to say. I always have time for the man I love."

"That's........what did you say ma?"

"I love you Damonte." she said and kissed him.

"I love you too Orchid....knew it for a while."

"Why not enlighten me?"

"I wanted to make sure our thing was official. I mean it when I say it." he said sitting on the couch and pulling her on his lap. "What you got on under this tee?"

"Panties, why?"

"I want 'em off." he said reaching under her shirt and snatching them off.

"Damn boy."

"I'll get you some new ones." he said now pulling her shirt over her head and taking her nipple between his teeth.

"Ummmm, I like that daddy." she moaned as he laid her back and spread her thighs.

"Is this daddy's pussy?" he asked between licks.

"Yes!" she moaned, arching her back.

"You love me?"

"Yes D! Yes…..I love you. Shit!" she moaned as he continued torturing her clit with his tongue.

They fucked like rabbits on the couch before falling to the floor to continue there. After multiple orgasms, they laid on the plush carpet wrapped in each other's limbs breathing hard. It was the best sex they'd ever had.

"That shit…..was intense." D said on a strangled breath.

"Unh huh!" Orchid moaned as she kissed down his chest.

"What you doing ma?"

"Mind your business." she said taking him in her mouth, awakening the sleeping giant. "Fuck! What got….into you?"

"You did." she said and started another wild session of off the hinges sex.

They were finally ready for an intermission, so D grabbed a sheet, wrapping both of them in it and lighting a blunt he'd rolled. He handed it to Orchid and kissed on her neck while she indulged.

"Do you know you're the best thing that's ever happened to me?" he asked staring into her eyes.

"Baby, that's sweet. I feel the same. Now that I have you, I can't imagine what my life would be like without you in it."

"That's what I needed to hear ma. I want you home with me….waiting for me naked when I walk through the door."

"D…we practically spend all our time at each other's houses anyway. You pretty much get that already."

"Nah, I want us to have our shit together, not two separate homes. I want you with me. We don't have to stay in my house; I'll buy a new one. Whatever you want. So, wsup?"

"D…….I'd love to live with you." she said kissing him. "Do I get to pick the house?!" she perked.

"Whatever you want ma." he said kissing her.

"Let's go get dressed and grab some grub before I wanna jump on that ass again. You done worked me to death."

"You liked it." she said heading towards the stairs naked just to tease him.

"Oh….I loved that shit. Matter of fact….." he said getting up. "Let me holler at you for a minute."

It didn't take long for Orchid to find a house and fall in love with it. D gave her complete control of decorating and furnishing the house and no budget restrictions. Whatever Orchid wanted she got. Not wanting to move in or have D see the house until it was finished, he was in the dark…but he trusted her. He did wish the process moved a lil faster though. Between her job and finishing the house, their quality time has been cut in half.

D was chillin' at Keon's crib smoking and counting money when Orchid called. More so because of his schedule, they hadn't seen each other in four days. He reached for his phone and instantly had a smile on his face. "I love you." he said.

"I love you too. What you doing?"

"Just handling something light. How was your day?"

"Good. I get to take a break for a minute."

"You quit!?" he asked trying not to sound too excited.

"No, you'd like that wouldn't you? I took a vacation. Two weeks of nothing, but hopefully sex and time with you."

"I can definitely help with that. So nothing huh….you done with the top secret house?"

"Actually smart ass, I am. I wanted to see if you had time to come take a look at where you'll be laying your head."

"Give me an hour and I'll be at your crib to scoop you. Love you ma."

"Love you."

"Ya'll niggas mushy as hell."

"Fuck you, that's love. Something you aint never gonna know about until you stop hoeing."

"Aww…..okay. You don't need no details or nothing but on the real…….I ain't been fucking nobody but Kiko. She got a hold on a nigga, I'm feeling her."

"Kiko's good peoples. If you gonna fuck with her you better make sure it's on the up and up. I'm not trying to be beefin' with Orchid over some shit you did."

"I got you man. It's all good."

Damonte was blown away by what Orchid did with the house. To him, it was perfect. It was done in earth tones with a modern feel and not too feminine. The bedroom even better, mahogany and black with silver accents. She took him through the guest rooms, his and her offices, dining room, kitchen......she definitely had good taste.

"And since my man is so good to me, I figured I'd do a lil something' something special for you. Blindfold please." she said handing it to him to put on. "No peeking, just follow me. I got you."

"I trust you.....lead the way."

She opened the basement door and carefully led D down the stairs. She couldn't stop smiling knowing he would love it. She placed him in the middle of the floor and stood in front of him. "Okay, I feel that every man's home is his sanctuary. But....living with a woman you sometimes need a sanctuary within your sanctuary. Now, don't let me have to come down here and drag you out by your ears. Got it?"

"I got you."

"Okay. I present to you, your very own boom boom room...designed by Orchid." she said taking off the blind fold.

She stood back, smiling while he raved about the room. She transformed the finished basement into his own lil man cave. He had the flat screen, video games, card table, stereo, theater style seating and with a private bath and a few plush perks.

"Now this over here, is not for any hoochies. This is for your own private show and there's only one rule."

"What's that?" he said kissing on her neck ready to

fuck in the sexy room.

"The only boom boom that goes on in here is with me." she said kissing him.

"That's a given. So…." he said pulling out a knot of bills. "……how about we test out the pole. See if you can make it do what it do."

"Right this way please." she stepped up to where the pole was mounted and sat him in a plush chair that was part of the mini stage. "Front row seating."

"I'm liking this already."

Chapter 7

D was missing in action from the streets the first few days after they'd moved into the house. They took their time christening every room in the house. Since Orchid was on vacation and they'd been lacking in the quality time department, he stayed home and conducted as much business as he could over the phone with Keon.

"Damn nigga....when Orchid gonna let you out the pussy?" Keon laughed.

"Nigga, if I had my way, I'd never leave that shit." he laughed. "Yo, my baby did the damn thing with the house. I guess I'll have ya'll niggas over."

"When? And tell Orchid to cook.....you got the one that can burn. Kiko need a lil practice. I ain't telling her that though." he laughed.

"You better not. "

"She makes up for the lack of skills in the kitchen in every other area. I was thinking about taking her to Vegas for a couple days when your ass get back."

"Nigga, that's why we got niggas working for us. Tell them niggas to handle that shit and we can all roll out. Orchid on vacation anyway."

"True dat."

"You handle that shit and I'll handle the arrangements for Vegas. We leave tomorrow."

"Aiight. Let me get on that right now.....cause the money gotta keep flowin'."

"Indeed nigga. Aiight, I'll hit you later."

D was sitting in his "boom boom" room smoking an L and watching Belly when Orchid came down the stairs wearing a thong, matching bra and stilettos. She licked her lips when D turned to look at her with lust in his eyes.

"Come her girl." he said putting his blunt down and welcomed her to his lap.

Orchid kissed him slowly giving him her tongue to play with.

"Damn! Now that's how you greet a nigga!"

"I love you daddy."

"I love you too ma."

"Yeah.....show me." she said unsnapping her bra and tossing it to the floor as he took her taut nipple in between his teeth, tickling her nipple with his tongue.

She pulled her thong to the side and inserted his hard dick into her dripping wet pussy, sliding down on it. She began grinding slowly before picking up her pace.

"Fuck! You.....so.....wet! Shit!" he said holding on to her hips unable to move.

"Is this my dick?" she said tightening her pussy around him.

"Yes....this shit is all.....yours. Fuck!" he yelled as she began picking up the pace, bouncing up and down on his dick. She felt him swell inside of her, so she knew he was getting ready to come.

"I'm....cumming ma. Pull out." he moaned as his warm man juices shot up in her. "Damn.....that nut was big." he said outta breath.

"This is just the intermission playa. I couldn't wait to have you in me. Now....I got something I want you to taste."

"What's gotten into you? A nigga loving that shit.....and I didn't have to pull out. What's up with that?"

"What's the use? The damage is already done." she said and smiled.

"Damage? What you......ma, you pregnant?" he

said and smiled.

"It seems like we may have did a little bit too much christening. I'm three weeks according to the doctor. Guess I got a hell of a housewarming gift."

"You having my seed ma?" he asked touching her face and looking into her tear filled eyes.

"Yes."

"Why you crying? You not happy? Well your man is fucking ecstatic! I'm gonna be a father!" he yelled. "Talk to me." he said holding her.

"I'm happy....but a little scared. I wasn't planning on having a baby this soon."

"So...."

".....but, I'm not alone. I'm having a baby by the man that I love....so yes, I'm happy."

"As long as your happy." he said and kissed her. "And no, you're not alone. I'll be here every step of the way. I love you ma."

"I love you too baby."

"Come on.....lets go upstairs so I can eat me some pregnant pussy and have some unprotected sex." he said getting up with her still attached to him. "I'm gonna put another one in ya, right now."

After making love and showering, Orchid went into the kitchen to start cooking dinner. She had her music pumping while she prepared the salmon to go into the oven. She was shaking her tail feather when D walked up behind her cupping her breasts.

"Don't get nothing started up again." she said and smiled.

"What?! Consider it started. Before we get into that, you feel like company tonight?"

"Who?"

"Keon and Kiko."

"Oh, I'm always down to hang with my bestie. I was thinking about giving her a key." Orchid laughed.

"As long as you don't mind her walking in on a porn in progress." he said opening her robe and sliding his hand into her panties until he found her clit.

"Oh….baby." she moaned. "What…..time they coming?"

"Couple hours." he answered between kisses. "Put that to the side so I can holler at my pussy a minute." he said pushing the food to the side and putting Orchid on the counter. He retrieved some whipped cream from the fridge, laid Orchid back and sprayed some all over her pussy.

"What are you doing?"

"Making a pussy sundae." he smiled and dove into her middle face first. He lapped at her clit through the whipped cream and sucked on it, causing Orchid to go crazy.

"Fuck! Eat…..this….pussy daddy." she moaned and through her pussy in his face.

D tortured her with his tongue until she began to shake and yell his name.

"Come on ma……let daddy get….that nut." he said and sucked on her clit until his face was coated with her juices. "Come here." he said pulling her to the end of the counter and sliding in her wet pussy.

"Damn! This…pussy….is good." he moaned stroking her.

He picked her up and leaned her against the wall, pounding her insides, causing her to scream out in ecstasy. His face twisted in pleasure as she began to work her pussy, which always drove him wild. He sucked on each breast as she moved around on his dick. Ready to do some more damage of his own, he took a step back, grabbed Orchids hips and began bouncing her on his dick. "Fuck! Do that….shit ma!" he said feeling himself about to nut. She offered him her tongue and he accepted as she moved around on his dick, milking him dry. "God! I fucking love you girl."

"I love you too baby. Now let me down, I gotta get the whipped cream out my pussy."

"You need help with that?" he asked and smiled.

"No….you can bleach the kitchen so I can finish cooking. I don't want our friends eating my juices."

"That's right….they're all for me."

After preparing dinner and making sure the house was clean, they still had some time before their friends would arrive. So, they took the opportunity to have a quickie. Even at this early in her pregnancy, her hormones were working overtime. She was always horny, sometimes starting alone before D made it to the house. After showering and putting on some leggings and one of D's t-shirts, Orchid curled up next to him on the couch watching a game while she waited for her friend to arrive.

'That smells good." Orchid said hinting at wanting some of the blunt he was smoking.

"That's all you gonna be doing from now on is smelling it. No weed, no drinks, no clubbing…"

"I'm not even showing yet and you talking about no clubbing."

"There's a lot of shit that can pop off in the club. If something happened to you or my seed, I'd have to go on a killing spree."

"I guess I can feel you on that…..can I at least smoke one last blunt with you, damn? And since I can't smoke, don't temp me….no smoking in the house."

"What?! Fuck it, I'll just smoke down here."

"I be in here, so you can't smoke in here either. Matter of fact….I changed my mind; this is your boom boom room."

"Thank you….I was 'bout to say."

"You're welcome. Just so you know, if you're smoking down here I'm not coming down here. That means no sex in the champagne room and no pole action."

"Come on ma." D whined.

"That's the door, gotta go." she said getting up and hopping up the stairs.

She opened the door with a Kool-Aid smile on her face and embraced her best friend. She held her tight, missing her although it'd only been a week. She punched Keon in the arm after giving her a wet kiss on her forehead.

"What it do O?" Keon asked, calling her by the nick name he gave her.

"Chillin' bout to smoke my last L with your bossy ass man."

"Your last? You giving up the bud?" Keon screeched.

"Yeah…..at least for eight months and a week." she answered and waited for her girl to catch on.

"Bitch! You pregnant!?" Kiko screamed.

"Yeah…found out today." Orchid smiled

"Ahhhh!" Kiko screamed and grabbed her friend tight.

"Okay….that's my cue to leave ya'll alone. I'll be in the man cave where there's some testosterone.

"Whatever! Girl, I'm so happy for you. How you feeling?" Kiko took her by the hand and led her to the couch.

"Pretty good....I stay horny now but other than that, I'm good. I was having mixed emotions at first."

"I know....you wanted to be married when you had kids. Maybe it'll happen."

"We haven't discussed marriage, so I don't know about that."

"Girl, D loves you to pieces, it'll happen. You tell your mom yet?"

"I just found out this afternoon. I figured I'd tell D first, since he helped and all."

"Smart ass. Let's call her....I got's to hear this."

"Fine" Orchid said grabbing the phone and putting it on speaker.

"Well shit...it's about time I heard from my child. I thought I was gonna have to come look for you." her mom laughed.

"I'm sorry mom; it's only been two days though."

"Hi Mom!" Kiko yelled.

"Hey baby. What are ya 'll doing....getting crunk?"

"Where'd you get that?" Orchid asked.

"BET. So, what's up?"

"Well....I have something to tell you."

"Oh Lord, let me sit down. Go ahead."

"Well.....I'm pregnant." she said and paused for her reaction.

"Pregnant? You're making me a grandma?"

"Yeah, I am."

"Awww baby! I'm so happy for you. How you feeling?"

"Pretty good. I hope I continue to feel that way."

"So when can we be expecting our bundle of joy?"

"Approximately May 30th. I'm glad I'll miss having to carry this load through the summer."

"I can't wait to meet him or her. You two better make sure ya'll asses is here for thanksgiving and I want pictures of every ultrasound, stretch mark…..everything."

"I will definitely do that."

"Is that your mom?" D said walking in and hearing her voice.

"Yeah it's me….your fertile ass." she said and laughed.

"I'm gonna call you in a few minutes mom. I need to holla at you for a minute."

"Alright. Ok baby, call me tomorrow. I love you guys."

"Love you too." Orchid and Kiko said in unison.

"Ma, I gotta make a run, I'll be back in a few. Here is your last L….you better enjoy it cause that's it."

"Yes father." she said and rolled her eyes.

Orchid and Kiko smoked the blunt of haze D gave her and got caught up on the latest in the hood and with each other. They were tore up giggling to no end until Kiko gasped.

"Girl….I almost forgot to tell you about your grimy ass cousin Shelle."

"What her ass up to? I've been calling her and she don't answer."

"That's because she too busy hatin on you. I ran into her the other day when I went around the way to my aunts' house. She was all "She don't know what to do with a man like D. He needs some of this…..he'll get tired of her boring ass and when he does….I'll be there to pick up where she fell short." Then the bitch wanted to jump bad with me. She lucky that's your family 'cause I was about to whip her ass."

"No the fuck her shady ass didn't! I should've

known....she was feeling some type of way that he asked her who I was instead of pushing up on her like she thought he was."

"What?!" Kiko fell out laughing. "You never told me that."

"Yeah girl. She was souped, switching all hard over to the car, and he was like "who's your girl?"" Orchid laughed.

"That's what her ass gets!" Kiko laughed. "You gonna say something to her?"

"What for? My belly will say all that needs to be said.....and her ass don't know he bought us this fly ass.....matter of fact. I think I may give a lil dinner party and invite her over."

"Let's call her now." Kiko said excitedly.

"Trouble maker" Orchid said slapping her. "Okay." she said picking up the phone and dialing Shelle's number from the house phone.

"Who dis?" Shelle answered in her usual ghetto manner.

"Damn bitch, you can't call your cousin back?"

"What up Orchid?! I was gonna call you girl."

"Uh huh....anyway, what you doing tomorrow?"

"Nothing as far as I know of, why wsup?"

"I'm gonna have a few people over for dinner and was calling to invite you."

"Oh okay, I'm there. This a new number?" she said looking at her id.

"Yeah...new house, new number."

"You moved?"

"Yeah....me and D brought a house about a half hour away."

"Oh" Shell said dryly. "Guess who I saw the other day and asked about you?"

"Who?"

"Preme. He said he was coming back to get what's his….your ass." Shelle said laughing.

"Shit! What we had is ancient history. I don't even wanna be friends with his lying ass."

"I heard that. Aiight well, what you drinking….I'll bring a bottle."

"Get whatever you drinking, I can't right now."

"What you on antibiotics or something?" Shelle laughed.

"No bitch…I'm pregnant." Orchid said and tried not to laugh when she heard her gasp.

"By D?"

"Who else am I gonna be pregnant by? Anyway, dinner is at 7 and tell your mom I said hi and I love her."

"Aiight….I'll see you tomorrow girl. Later." she said and hung up before Orchid could say anything else.

When she hung up the phone, she and Kiko burst out laughing. Orchid laughed so hard her stomach was hurting. "Girl….that shit was hilarious!" she said still laughing.

"Do you think she'll come?"

"Yeah….just to be nosey and talk shit but I got something for that ass." Orchid said still laughing.

"So…..I get to be the god mother of the baby right?" Kiko smiled

"Auntie and god mother, so we'll be expecting two gifts."

"Gifts for who?" D asked walking through the living room with Keon on his heels.

"Damn you nosey!" Kiko said to D.

"You should talk." Keon said sitting next to Kiko on the couch. "Ma, we staying over and leaving in the morning."

"Why? Not that I mind."

"Because we are."

"These are for you ma." D said handing Orchid a bouquet of roses.

"Thank you baby." Orchid leaned her head back to kiss him until she felt something hit her in the leg. "What's this?"

"Open it and see. Geesh…women." Keon laughed.

"Shut up." Kiko punched him in his leg.

"Oh my God!" Orchid gasped looking at the flawless princess cut diamond and platinum ring she held in her hand. "D….."

"Ma…..I knew from the day I laid eyes on you, that you were the one. I already planned on making you my wife…but with a baby on the way, I wanted to do it now. So…..Orchid, the love of my life…..will you be my wife?" he asked taking the ring and dropping to one knee.

"I…….D, this is…."

"You making me nervous ma." he laughed a nervous laugh.

"Wow, this is the first time since I've known her that she's been speechless." Kiko laughed.

"Well……."

"Yes……of course I'll marry you." she struggled to get out through tears. "I can't believe you did this."

"Believe it baby…..you're all I need. I love you." he said sliding the ring on her finger.

"I love you too." she said and kissed him.

"Hell yeah!" he yelled getting up and lifting her into the air.

"Hey….I'm pregnant remember."

"My bad. Aiight K, let's get the champagne flowing. You miss…can only have a small glass."

"…and a half blunt. I shared with Kiko so

technically it was only a half blunt I smoked."

"Gotta love it dawg." Keon laughed.

Orchid woke up the next morning with a smile on her face and couldn't stop smiling. She showered and made breakfast for everyone before going out on errands for the dinner she was making that night. She couldn't wait to see Shelle's face when she laid eyes on her engagement ring.

"There's my future wife." D came up behind her kissing on her neck. "You up and dressed already…where you going?"

"Going to the store to pick up a few things for the dinner tonight."

"Nah….I want you to relax. What you trying to serve?"

"Something simple…maybe soul food."

"You and Kiko go relax…do girl stuff. I'mma call up my people's restaurant and have them hook us up. I don't want you doing too much….matter of fact, you need to quit your job and stay home."

"Not this again. Baby, I enjoy working and having my own money."

"My money is your money ma…..and we got more than enough. Just think about it for me."

"I'll think about it."

"I'll take that. Who's coming over?"

"The two already here, I invited Shell and Shaunie too."

"My mom is coming. You know she wants to see you after I told her the news."

"The more the merrier." she said wrapping her arms around his neck and kissing him. "Have I told you how much I love you?"

"No….but you show me every day. I love you."

"I love you too. Oh....Kiko told me yesterday that Shell was talking shit."

"About...?"

"Me. I don't know what to do with a man like you and when you get tired of my boring ass she'll be there to scoop you up. Let me know she's digging you like that." Orchid laughed.

"Ma, that shit ain't even funny. Me and Shell cool peoples and that's all the fuck it's ever gonna be. Besides.....I ain't going nowhere." he grabbed a hand full of ass.

"She also brought my ex up. Said she saw him and he asked about me....said he was coming back to get what's his."

"Fuck outta here! Don't let it be no shit Orchid." D said now smirking.

"You ain't gotta check me nigga. I told you all the shit I went through with his retarded ass before. Do you really think I wanna sign up for that shit again?" she raised her voice.

"I ain't mean it like that ma." he held her. "Just the thought of another nigga even thinking about trying to get at someone that's mine.....got me tripping. Your ex.....that's that nigga Supreme right?"

"Arsenio you mean?"

"Arsenio?! Get the fuck outta here!" D fell out laughing. "Wow....his mom must not like his ass."

"Who cares, the only man I'm concerned with is my future husband." she said kissing him.

"Let me holla at you in the boom boom room for a minute."

Chapter 8

By 6pm their guest were arriving. Shaunie, Kiko, and Keon and D's mom were the first guests to arrive. Orchid was excited because this was her first time meeting D's mom face to face. They'd talked on the phone a lot, but he'd never taken her over to her home since she had a husband he didn't get along with. Orchid was a little embarrassed by how much she was fussing over her. Right before dinner time is when Shelle showed up.

"What up cousin?......and Kiko." she mumbled.

"Hey. Come on in, we're about to eat." Orchid said closing the door and showing her in.

"This is a nice house. You do all the decorating?"

"Yeah. Took me a lil while, but I got it done." she said stopping when the doorbell rang. "Go ahead in the dining room, I'll be right there." Orchid said heading back to the door. "Mom!" she yelled. "What are you doing here?"

"My future son in law paid for my ticket and told me to get out here."

"Oh, so you knew about the engagement?"

"He called and asked me before he asked you. He recognizes my gangsta." she said and laughed.

"Let me take your bags. Everyone is in the dining room, I'll be right there."

The night was filled with laughter and music with a little hateration in the air but overall, it was a success. D's mom and Orchid's mom were drinking and talking like old friends and that made their night. The last thing Orchid and D wanted was family drama.

"I see you with some bling on girl. When'd you get that?" Shell said picking up Orchids hand admiring her ring.

"Last night.....it was a total shock, but I'm happy about it." Orchid beamed.

"Where'd you get it?"

"Who buys their own engagement ring? You need to ask D where he brought it." Kiko added with a chuckle knowing she was fuming.

"Engagement ring?"

"Yeah...."

"Well, I guess we should make a couple of announcements now then huh?" D said over hearing their conversation.

"What announcements?" Shell asked ready to snap.

"Well......for those of you who don't know, me and Orchid have a few things happening. First.....we are expecting our first seed around the end of May." he said and stopped while their family and friends cheered. "And......last night, Orchid made me the luckiest nigga on earth when she said yes to being my wife!" he said holding up the sparkler she wore on her finger. "So.....fill your glasses.....this is a celebration!"

They spent the rest of the evening celebrating, which turned into a sleepover. After D's mom made the men clean up, Orchid and Kiko got everyone set up in the guests' rooms. Around 1am is when everyone retired to their rooms, finally giving Orchid and D some alone time. After a quickie in the shower, they laid in the bed in each other's arms.

"I love you ma."

"I love you too baby."

"You know we have to have an engagement party."

"I guess we can do that. Can I drink?"

"Hell no!"

"It was worth a try."

D wasted no time putting together an engagement party fit for royalty….street royalty. Orchid was four months and was sporting the cutest belly. She also gave in and resigned from her job after repeated debates over it, but not until after he agreed there would be no bullshit from him when she wanted to go back after the baby.

While Orchid went to pick her mother up from the airport, D stopped at the venue to make sure everything was on point before going home to grab their bags and meet Orchid and her mother back at the hotel where the party was being held and all their guests were staying. Walking through the lobby, he bumped into Shell who was on her way up to her room.

"Wsup D." she said smiling flirtatiously.

"What up Shell? You straight?"

"I'm good, getting ready to go upstairs, get my smoke on. You got time for an L?"

"Nah, I need to get back to the house and then back here before Orchid gets back from the airport."

"Oh…aiight." she said with a smirk.

"I'll check you later."

"Aiight."

"Bitch" he mumbled walking away.

Every since Orchid told him about her remarks he wasn't feeling her. He also found out that Preme had indeed been looking for Orchid and she was seen kicking it with him. Preme was shady, he knew that personally. Put them two together and it was a recipe for disaster.

By eight o'clock the ballroom was filled with their guests. They had a mixture of everyone there, hustlers, entertainers, and most importantly their friends and family. After giving Orchid multiple orgasms, which he loved about her being pregnant, they got dressed and went downstairs to make their entrance.

"Introducing the future Mr. and Mrs. Dewitt! Damn she fine dog!" their guest DJ yelled over the mic.

"You better watch that shit!" D laughed and yelled. They made their rounds around the ballroom greeting their guest and a few tag alongs. The drinks were flowing, the music was bumping and out of respect for the parents and Orchid there was no smoking in the ballroom but D arranged to have the conference room next to the ballroom to be transformed into a smoker lounge.

"Ma….me and the crew going to put something in the air. You aiight?"

"I'm good….go." she said kissing him and taking a seat at the table with her mom and D's.

She and Kiko sat at the table laughing and joking with the mothers until they saw Shell come in. The fact that Shell walked in wasn't the shocker, who she had on her arm was.

"Is that…..is that that low down piece of no good shit Arsenio with Shell?" Orchids' mom yelled.

"Looks like it is mom."

"Your cousin is beyond foul. Preme…..of all niggas to walk up in here with. This can't turn out good." Kiko said.

"It's not a problem unless you let it become one baby." Orchids' mom said putting her arm around her.

"Am I missing something?" D's mom asked.

"I'm sorry Mama Debbie. That's my cousin Shell and the man she's with is my ex. He's trouble and it looks like she is trying to start some."

"You and him haven't been......" she began to ask.
"He and I have been apart for almost four years.
He's been in prison and if he wasn't, I'd still have
nothing else to do with him. He's the worst kind of
man there is....I just had to learn that the hard way.
Your son knows all about him."
"Forgive me if I offended you."
"Not at all, I have nothing at all to hide. I share
everything with your son as well as the other people
I love."
"I'm glad to know that and be included in that
group." she said and smiled.
"Where is D anyway?" Orchid's mom asked.
"He went to go smoke." she answered her.
"Actually, here he comes now." Kiko pointed.
"Why ya'll looking so serious over here?"
"That's why?" Kiko said and pointed in the
direction of Shelle and Preme. "No the fuck.....!
What's up with your cousin ma? She's a straight
hater, which is cool....we brush them off. Now her
ass is trying to start problems. First she tried to get
me to her room earlier....now this."
"She did what?!" the ladies asked in unison.
"Oh, hell no!" Orchid yelled getting up.
"Unh uh ma.....you pregnant." D said sitting her
down and squatting in front of her. "I don't want
anyone but you, so that shit didn't work. As far as
that nigga goes, I'll handle him."
"Besides, I've been wanting to whip your cousin's
ass for years, so please.....let me do it." Kiko said
seriously but laughing.
"Look, let's just enjoy the party, let Shell play
herself. Matter of fact.....yo K!" D yelled. "Help me
handle these ladies on the dance floor. Let's go!"
	Although a smile covered D's face, he was

in plot mode. He knew with Preme showing up with Shell that he was gonna be a problem. He trusted Orchid but he didn't trust his ass, so he was gonna keep a close eye on Orchid….knowing he'd be lurking not too far behind. The DJ played the first song he and Orchid danced to at the club, so he traded off partners and got it in with his wife.

"Go head ma!" he said as Orchid dropped it like it's hot….belly and all.

They were having a ball until Shelle walked over with her fake smile and cheesy gift.

"Heyyyyyy! Congratulations!" she said hugging Orchid and D. "Oh…wsup Kiko"

"Whatever bitch!" Kiko spat back

"What?! You better watch who the fuck you talking to." Shell shot back.

"Why is that? You's a scandalous ass bitch, and you supposed to be her family….."

"Kiko…" Orchid tried to intervene.

"Nah….let that shit go down.

"Aint shit going down." Shelle said with a smirk.

"See, what you don't know…is I've never liked your ass. The only reason I haven't fucked you up is because of my girl. However, all bets are off! Don't let me see your ass outside of here 'cause I will be fucking you up. Just nasty." Kiko said turning her nose up at Shelle.

"Fuck ya'll I'm outta here."

"Oh, don't forget to take your date with you bitch!" Kiko yelled.

"Ya'll can have him."

"Oh one more thing…" Orchid started. "When I drop this load…..that ass is mine. You trying my man? You done really fucked up."

"Whatever bitch…..I'll see ya'll asses around, I'm

going to my room."

"Actually, you're not. Our money paid for that room. The bellman has your shit and your key ain't gonna work. Bounce!"

After Shelle left the evening continued without a hitch. Champagne and Henny Black were flowing like water....everyone was having a ball. D and Keon stood by and watched admiringly with everyone else as Orchid and Kiko did their thing on the dance floor. All that mattered to D was that Orchid was happy, it was the least he could do with her giving him so much. No one realized Preme was still in the room and watching Orchid's every move. He looked at her belly and instantly became furious....she was supposed to have *his* baby. After tossing back a few shots he'd seen enough and needed to make his presence felt. He dismounted the bar stool and walked over to Orchid who was talking to a couple of her guests.

"So.....a nigga's gone for a few years and you go get pregnant and engaged huh?"

"What I do is no longer any of your business and you were not invited. Your date left.....you should've left with her."

"Man...fuck your scandalous ass cousin, she ain't my date. She was just a means for me to get to you. So....you really lovin' this nigga huh?"

"Are you fucking retarded? I'm having his baby....this is our engagement party. Lovin' him......nah, I'm in love with him. Why? Because he does for me all the things I could never get out of you. One of the main things......he's faithful."

By that time things were starting to get heated and Kiko headed over towards Orchid, texting Keon while in route.

"You's a cold ass bitch Orchid, I thought we had something."

"Nigga….what is you smoking?! Even before you went to prison we were over. You didn't know how to treat me when you had me and for that….you lost me. I'm trying to be nice and not call D over here, so why don't you take advantage of that and leave." she said turning her back on him.

"Bitch….don't you turn your back on me." he said grabbing her arm and slapping her across the face.

"Mother fucker!" Orchid said and punched him.

"Orchid….no!" Kiko yelled jumping in front of her and catching the fist that was intended for her.

"You hit like a bitch!" Kiko said returning the punch causing him to stagger.

"Oh, I got something for that ass!" Preme said pushing Kiko to the side and grabbing up Orchid.

"You better think the fuck again nigga!" D said through clench teeth.

"What?! This bitch and me got unfinished business…..so step the fuck off."

"Did this nigga……" D started before pushing Orchid to the side and knocking teeth out of Preme's face.

"Ma…what the fuck happened to your…..no this nigga didn't." Keon said and jumped on Preme's ass.

Before Orchid could gather herself, D's whole crew was stomping on Preme's ass and dragging him towards the door. Although Orchid was concerned about D getting arrested or maybe even killing Preme, she was too upset to do anything. She took a look at Kiko's eye and just cried.

"Oh my God! Look what he did to you!" she cried hugging her best friend. "Give me some ice!" she yelled at the bartender and placing it on her eye. "You okay? I can't believe you jumped in front of a punch for me."

"You're my girl and carrying my god child....that shit was not going down. I love you girl.....and you would've done the same for me."

"In a minute.....maybe we should call it the night. Since we both have shiners and all."

D was breathing fire when Keon pulled him off of Supreme. He wanted to kill that nigga but knew it wasn't the time or place for it....but he was gonna catch Preme's pussy ass.

"Come on yo! We need to go check on the ladies!" Keon yelled pulling him away.

"Shit! Where's Orchid?" D asked rushing back into the ballroom to find her, but was stopped by both their mothers.

"Damonte Lavar....what the fuck is all this shit going on?! Orchid and Kiko are sitting over there with black eyes and you have blood on you!" his mom yelled.

"Ma....I need to go check on Orchid real quick and no I didn't kill anyone."

"Was that the guy that trifling ass niece of my came in with?"

"Yeah....Shell always got some shit poppin off! I'mma handle this shit but we need to get Orchid upstairs."

When D and Keon got to the bar Kiko and Orchid were sitting there icing each other's eyes. When D walked up on them Orchid turned to look at him. The sight of the bruises on her face made his heart hurt and pisses him off even more.

"Ma.....I am so sorry this...."

"D....it's not your fault, my cousin and ex are

assholes. I just wanna go upstairs and put a steak on my eye......and Mayweather's over here."

"Boo.....look at your fucking eye!" Keon yelled.

"Fuck this shit!" he said turning to go back outside to look for Preme to finish his ass off.

"K! Just leave it alone right now. All I want is a bed, an ice pack, and to be in your arms."

"I can handle that....but that nigga is mine."

Chapter 9

The next couple of days D would not let Orchid leave the house. He ordered her to get some rest before she was up and running again. He also wanted to buy some time to find Preme. He knew from what went down at the party that they hadn't seen the last of him.

A couple of months had gone by and they was still no sign of Preme. Christmas was approaching and he wanted to do something special for Orchid. She had diamonds, cars, money…so he needed a grand gesture. Working by phone and internet with a realtor D purchased a villa in Barbados as Orchid's Christmas gift. A couple weeks before the holiday approached, he told her he had to go out of town for business, but what he did was fly out to check on the property.

He walked in the spacious home and was thoroughly impressed. It was fit for his queen, equipped with state of the art everything. A nursery, five bedrooms, Jacuzzi, heated pool, guest house and a nursery filled with the best for his lil man. After smoking an L, he left out to make arrangements for the other surprise he had planned, did some shopping and went back to the house to chill and check on home.

"How you feeling ma?"

"I'm ok. I'd be even better if your son would stop standing on my fucking bladder."

"Awww….you let him know his pops is gonna holler at him about that." he said still tickled that they were having a boy. "I'll be back early tomorrow. What you doing today?"

"Exactly what I'm doing now….watching movies

with Kiko and stuffing my face."

"Sounds like a plan. Ya'll enjoy….tell Kiko I said wsup."

"I will. I love you."

"I love you too ma."

Christmas morning and D hadn't slept at all. He was excited….nervous but never been more sure of anything in his life. He sat on the sofa in their oversized, plush bedroom and watched Orchid sleep. It was eight am and he needed to get her up if they were going to catch their flight in time.

"Ma…..wake up." D gently shook her.

"D……." she said turning over. "…..it's eight o'clock. Why are you bothering me?" she whined.

"Ma….we got moves to make. I'll explain everything later but I need you to get up and get dressed."

"You know what……this better be damn good." Orchid said tossing the covers off of her.

By ten o'clock they were at the airport boarding a flight to Barbados. D kept smiling from ear to ear and couldn't stop.

"What has got you all giddy?" Orchid asked.

"I can't be happy because it's Christmas and I'm with the people I love?"

"Nice try. Barbados is a reason to smile. Thank you babe."

"Oh….you ain't seen nothing yet."

Orchid slept almost the whole flight and then again in the car. Pregnancy was definitely kicking her ass. Kiko gazed out the window trying to eavesdrop on the conversation the men were having but had no success. Before she was about to bogart the conversation, she was mesmerized by the beautiful home they'd just pulled in front of.

"This shit is hot!" she perked. "Is this where we're staying......and does my bathroom have a Jacuzzi?" she laughed.

"What are you squawking about?" Orchid stretched.

"This house! It kinda reminds me of that dudes mansion from Belly."

"It does a little. Babe, is this a hotel or someone's house?" she asked following him to the door.

"It's not just someone's house.....it's our house." he said and waited for her response as he opened the door.

"Get the fuck outta here!" Orchid laughed.

"I'm serious ma....this is ours. Let me give ya'll the tour." he said leading the way around the spacious, luxurious villa.

"When did you do all of this?" Orchid asked with tears in her eyes.

"When I was out of town. It was part business, part pleasure."

"This is beautiful baby. I love you."

"I love you too. And what's beautiful, is we can come here and spend as much time as we want."

"Please, with you hollering in the cell at your peoples?"

"You ain't tell her dog?" Keon asked bouncing on the bed.

"Tell me what?"

"You man is officially out the business."

"D.....are you serious? I'm happy.....but how do you feel? You know how you like to ball."

"Ma...we better than good. Besides, I get a little.....let's call it a finders' fee for hooking my peoples up. Anyway....let's change and eat this dinner I got hooked up out back."

Resisting the urge to ask a hundred questions, Orchid put on the beautiful white linen dress and sandals D had laid out for her. She was in the mirror applying her final touches when she felt D's lips on her neck.

"You know I can't wait to make you my wife, right?" he said still kissing her neck.

"And I can't wait for you to be my husband." she turned around and kissed his lips. "You're my heart D….and not because of what you can give me, but because of who you are."

"Well…..let's do this then."

Orchid was moved to tears when she walked into the already beautiful backyard and it was set up for a wedding. She was also shocked to see her mother standing at the altar with the justice of the peace. Orchid walked down the aisle to Anthony Hamilton's "The Point of It All." D always said the song poured out all the feelings her had for her, and dubbed it their theme song.

There was not a dry eye, with the exception of Keon, as the ceremony took place. After the brief ceremony, they were introduced as Mr. and Mrs. Damonte Dewitt. The small group danced and drank the night away in celebration of the two souls becoming one.

"You know the best is yet to come for us…..right?" D asked as he held Orchid close.

Two months later, Orchid gave birth to Damonte Lavar Dewitt Jr. He weighed in at 8 pounds 2 ounces costing Orchid a few stitches down below. Although her labor was slightly difficult, she made it through having her mom, best friend, and her husband by her side.

"You will never touch me again without some form of birth control." Orchid said to D after getting cleaned up and holding her son.

"Don't be like that ma. We already agreed on three...four kids." D said and laughed.

"Well, it's not written anywhere on paper so I can deny it all I want to. Shit, it might be a minute before you get any. I may have flashbacks of what your dick did to me." Orchid said and cracked a smile.

"You know you love my dick ma." D said kissing her.

"Yeah, I sure do." she said wrapping her arms around his neck kissing him back.

"Hey, hey, hey....that's how ya'll got that one in there tearing up the nursery. My grandson is the most precious lil thing." Orchid's mom whined.

"Speaking of precious....let me go call the fam that ain't here. I got so caught up I forget to call my mom."

"Boy...." Theresa smacked him in the back of the head.".....that's for your mama cause she ain't here to do it. Get out there and call your mother and the rest of your family." she shook her head.

"Damn....your mom hit like Tyson." D laughed rubbing his head. "You need anything while I'm gone ma?"

"A blunt, but they won't let me have that in here." Orchid chuckled. "Other than that, I'm good."

After a short stay in the hospital, D and Theresa arrived to take Orchid and the baby home. After stopping at the grocery store to stock up on the formula that the baby would be on they walked through the door with their newest addition to the family. Orchid laid a sleeping DJ in his bassinet and sat on the couch, feeling relieved to have her body back to herself. She and her mom were cooing over all the pictures she'd taken of the baby when D walked in carrying a bottle of champagne and two blunts on a tray.

"See…..that's why I love you but I can't drink that and get up with the baby."

"Actually, I'm gonna get the baby tonight so you can get a good nights' rest. You're gonna need it baby. So, go ahead and enjoy……but you ain't smoking that mess in here around my grandson."

"We can go in the office but first…..a toast. To my new wife, mother in law and the best gift you could ever give me…..our son. I love you ma."

"I love you too." Orchid said and touched her glass with his.

"Aiight, ya'll go 'head….and save me a lil something to pull on."

"Let me know moms smoke." D laughed.

"I'm not professional like ya'll but I like to puff on the magic dragon every now and again."

"That's wsup. Come on baby mama."

Chapter 10

A year later and life was sweet for D and his family. Dj was getting big and already tearing around the house. D was enjoying being at home with DJ and was even happier that he'd talked Orchid into being a stay- at- home mom. Knowing she gave up her career for family, he made sure that anything she wanted, she got. Unfortunately, everyone didn't feel that way.

After being talked into it, Orchid kissed DJ and left out to met up with Kiko. They were going to the club for the first time in what seemed like ages. D and Keon were already together and promised to meet up with them at the club later on.

Once inside, Orchid and Kiko headed to VIP ordering a bottle of Henny Black with a champagne chaser. The club was slowly packing and the DJ was doing his thing, so the dance floor was full. Instead of jumping into the mix they chilled. Besides, Kiko had some news she was anxious to share.

"Aiight girl, spill."

"What?!" Kiko asked innocently.

"Bitch please. I know you better than you know yourself, so I know you got something to say….so let's hear it. Wait, let's have a shot first."

"Only champagne for me thanks."

"Uhhhhh….okay. So wsup?"

"I found out today that I'm pregnant." Kiko said and smiled widely.

"What!? Oh my God! I'm gonna be an auntie! I'm so happy for you girl." Orchid hugged her.

"Thank you. I'll be counting on you to help me through it."

"You know I got you. Soooo…..is Keon happy?"

"He doesn't know."

"Why not? Please don't tell me we gotta go to Maury."

"Hell no!" Kiko yelled and laughed. "I want to tell him face to face and I haven't seen him all day."

"Phew! Okay. With the baby on the way you might wanna move. You're not in the hood, but you're close enough to it."

"Actually, that's the other thing. Keon bought us a house and we move in three weeks."

"Damn! You really been holding out on a sister."

"I wanted to tell you face to face. You know what the best part is…..it's in your neighborhood."

"It damn sure is the best part! Let's toast…….to being neighbors and mommys."

"What ya'll ladies got to toast about." Preme said standing over their table sporting a scar left on his face from the last time he fucked with Orchid.

"You know damn well your ass needs to be as far away from me as possible."

"Why….because that's what you want or because of your man?" he smiled cockily.

"Nigga, first….that's my husband. Second, like I told you before you went to prison I didn't want anything to do with you."

"Husband?! You married that nigga?!"

"Who's married?! Oh……hey Orchid and friend."

"This bitch." Kiko sighed.

"What? We can get there bitch!" Shelle spat.

"Kiko…..be easy." Orchid said pushing her back towards her seat. "What the fuck is your problem Shelle? She aint did shit to you and neither have I….. you can keep the fuck moving with your hating ass."

"Hating? Oh, I'm hating because your boyfriend is a big time dealer? No….I must be hating because of the big house you have that I've only been invited to once."

"Bitch all of the above. The only problem with that statement is that D is my husband and what business he may or may not be in is none of your business. Both of ya'll get the fuck away from my table before it's a problem."

"It already is." D walked up with flared nostrils. "Didn't I tell your ass before nigga? You hard of hearing or do you want your ass whipped again or worse?"

"I'mma step…..but I'll be seeing your ass nigga." Preme said walking away with Shelle on his heels.

"That nigga must have a death wish……and Shelle! Baby, you should've chin checked her ass. I know she started some shit." Keon said sitting next to Kiko and kissing her.

"Actually…..I can't fight in my condition."

"Damn! Ya'll ain't been here long and you drunk already?" Keon laughed. "Lightweight."

"Actually, I'm not drunk……I'm pregnant." Kiko said and smiled.

"You still should've……what you say?"

"I'm pregnant. Found out today."

"You………..woo! What…..what! Nigga, you hear that?! I'm having a baby!" Keon shouted, swinging at the air. "I love you ma. Why you ain't tell me earlier?"

"I wanted to tell you face to face. You happy?"

"What?! My ass is ecstatic times three. Shit, I been pounding that pussy overtime trying to put one in you since my nephew been born."

"You're just nasty." Orchid laughed.

"Nasty? Shit, I'm trying to put another one up in your fine ass." D said kissing her. "Let's go do our thing....give them a lil time alone." he said noticing K and Kiko kissing and having a moment.

After making sure all the final arrangements were in place with his supplier, Keon and the rest of his crew, D decided it was time for a change of scenery. Orchid was not having being away from Kiko and her family at first but after constant persuasion and Kiko promising to visit frequently, she agreed. They purchased a home in the 'burbs of New York State. There former home was too big for just the three of them but the new home was ridiculous. Not one to sit idle for too long, D opened up a shop and sold top of the line rims, audio and anything else you could need to give your car a lil something extra.

It took a few months for them to get settled and comfortable but they'd settled in nicely. The only thing missing from Orchids life were the people she was used to seeing every day. Knowing Orchid was lonely, he decided to pick up a lil surprise for her on his way home from the shop.

"It took you long enough to get home. You know DJ can only keep me entertained but for so long." Orchid pouted without looking up from the TV.

"It's a sad day when you need your son to keep you company." Kiko said and smiled.

"Oh shit!" Orchid yelled and ran to hug her friend. "Awww....look at your belly." she said rubbing circles around Kiko's small basketball. "How you been feelin'?"

"Let's just say I now know what you were talking about. Sharing your body with someone is not fun at all. I told Keon he ain't getting no more after this one."

"I heard that. Where is your baby daddy?"

"D dropped me off and took him to go see the shop."

"Good….we can have some girl talk. So….how's everything been?" Orchid asked pulling her to the couch and sitting down.

"It's been good. Keon has been so overprotective and clingy that it annoys the shit outta me. It's sweet though. I miss ya'll like crazy. And where is my god son?"

"He's with my mother for the weekend. Since we're near a major airport, she hops on one and comes to visit like she around the corner."

"Hey, when you a big baller like her you can do that." Kiko said and laughed. "I know you got some weed around here…let me get a few pulls before the warden comes back."

"I got you."

By the time D and Keon arrived back at the house, dinner was cooked and the ladies were sitting around talking shit and watching movies. It's something they'd both missed doing. They were miserable without each other, but knew that life may take them in different directions.

"Look at you looking like you never had a baby. Give me some love girl!" Keon yelled hugging Orchid.

"That's enough, you got your own."

"How you doing daddy to be?"

"Good. As long as I have my lady and my seed….all is good. I smell it in the air; ya'll better not be getting my daughter high." Keon laughed.

"Daughter!? All the shit we been sitting here talking

and you aint tell me bitch!?" Orchid slapped her.
"I was going to…damn."

Orchid had the best time she'd had in a while the next three days. She and Kiko shed a few tears when it was time for them to hug good bye. D knew she was missing back home, shit….so was he. He made a mental note to make sure they went back and visited frequently so the home sickness didn't set in too bad.

"You okay ma?" he asked hugging Orchid.
"Yeah. I just miss her, that's all."
"I know. We'll go back soon for a long visit. What time your mom bringing my lil soldier home?"
"Your lil soldier is already home and upstairs napping. When he gets up, you can go in there and put away all the shit his grandma sent back with him."
"Damn! She at it again?"
"Yup." Orchid said getting up.
"Where you going?"
"To take a shower and then to the mall. Your sons' new purchases made me jealous, so I have to shop."
"How about I help you with that shower and we can all go?"
"If you help me with my shower I may need help with something else." she said leaning over, offering him her tongue and sticking her hand in his pants.
"Mmmmm….I'll race your ass to that motherfucka!"

Orchids' birthday rolled around and she wasn't exactly feeling like celebrating. She missed Kiko and Jersey period. The bright spot of her life and the reason for her happiness now was her husband and son….but D had been out the house a lot more. She packed up DJ to drop off at daycare and headed to the salon for a day of pampering. She knew D would have something up his sleeve and figured she should be ready. Just as she was about to walk out the door, D came through it carrying a bouquet of flowers and a few bags.

"Hey ma. Happy Birthday!" he said kissing her and handing her the flowers.

"Thank you baby. Been shopping huh?"

"You know I gotta hook my wife up. Where you going?"

"To drop DJ off and to the salon. I'll be back in a couple of hours."

"Not so fast." he said picking up DJ "Right lil man?"

"Yes!" DJ said loudly.

"What's up?"

"D….you wanna go with grandma, so I can take mommy to Jersey for the weekend to do it up?"

"Yeah! Grandma!" he said and clapped his lil hands.

"What….we going back to Jersey?" Orchid beamed.

"Yup. I figured since your girl can party now, you'd like it. I know ya'll miss each other. Besides, I can't wait to see my niece in person." D said referring to three week old Keona.

"Me either. So….when do we leave?"

"In about an hour. Your mom is meeting us at the airport to take lil man and we getting on our flight."

"Thank you baby. This is so thoughtful of you."

"You know I make it do what it do."

They hadn't sold their home in Jersey, so that's where they stayed. Walking through the door they were both flooded with memories. Orchid missed her house and Jersey but she had to do what she needed to make her husband happy, even if she was a lil lonely.

"What you thinking about?" D asked wrapped his arms around her.

"How much I miss this house….and Jersey. And how you got me pregnant as soon as we moved in."

"I was thinking about that too." D smiled at the memories. "Ma….are you that unhappy in New York?"

"It's not that I'm unhappy…..I have you and our son. But I do miss this house, our friends…..Jersey is all I know. I do know that times and people change, so I'm rolling with the punches."

"That's why I love you….you're my ride or die. But ma, if you wanna come back….we can. I miss it too." he confessed.

"Baby, we got the shop and the house out there. I just have to suck it up."

"You don't have to suck anything up. I want whatever makes you happy….I mean that."

"I know you do." she said wrapping her arms around his neck and kissing him.

"So…..what can I do to make you happy?"

"Right now…….you can take me upstairs and make love to me before you drop me at a salon to get my wig split."

"That I can do."

Orchid enjoyed her birthday more than she had in a while. She was in Jersey and she was able to get it in old school style with her best friend. The joy from her birthday followed her back home and D noticed how happy she was. That made his decision easy, they were going back to Jersey…..but not before spending some time in Barbados.

As soon as they stepped off the plane D's cell was blowing up.

"What up K?" D answered with a smile on his face that quickly turned dark.

"Yo….the shit done hit the fan down here dog."

"What up?"

"That bitch ass nigga Preme had some of his goons run up in the stash spot. We bodied a couple of them niggas but his ass….is going down."

"Oh, you know I got some unfinished business with that pussy anyway. Look, we just got back from the islands…I'm at the airport now. Give me a few hours and I'll be there."

"Aiight….I got everything we need already here."

"Aiight my nig….one." he said and ended the call.

"Fuck!" he said out loud.

"What's wrong baby?"

"That mother fucker Preme is out there causing problems for K. I gotta go check this shit out."

"Well, let me go with you."

"Nah…..you and the baby go home. We'll be back out in Jersey soon enough. I'll back home tomorrow at the latest."

"You be careful daddy."

"Always."

"Oh…I forgot, I got you a lil souvenir."

"From Barbados?"

"Nah…..Jersey. I'm pregnant." she said and smiled.

"Are you serious?" D beamed.

"Yeah. I took a home test but I have to go to the doctors to get it confirmed."

"You know you make me the happiest nigga alive." he said hugging her with DJ in their arms.

"Kiss….kiss." DJ cheered.

"Oh, trust me lil man…I am. Look, I'm gonna try to get back tonight so we can celebrate. Don't be in my shit…smoking yourself retarded Orchid."

"I got you."

"Yeah….you sure do. I love you ma."

"I love you too."

Chapter 11

Orchid waited up until 2 am for D to get home, but he still hadn't arrived. After calling his phone and getting his voicemail, she left him a message and fell asleep. At almost four in the morning her phone and doorbell rang at the same time. She grabbed her cell seeing it was Kiko and answered as she was on her way to the door.

"Hey...."

"Oh my God!......Oh God!" Kiko cried into the phone.

"Kiko....what's going on? Hold on, someone's at the door."

When Orchid opened the door to find the police on the other side, her heart hit the floor.

"Can I help you?" she asked.

"Are you Mrs. Dewitt?" the black officer asked.

"I am.....how can I help you?"

"You mind if we step inside?" the other black officer flashed his badge.

"May I ask what is this about?" she asked completely forgetting Kiko was still on the phone in her hand.

"Uh....there's no easy way to say this but......we were notified by a department in Jersey that your husband.....was murdered a couple of hours ago."

"Nooooooo!" she screamed dropping to the floor. "Nooo! He can't be...we're having a baby!" she cried.

"Mrs. Dewitt....I am so sorry for your loss. Is there someone we can call that can come be with you?"

"I....I......" she was unable to speak or even process what she'd just heard, but she knew it was real.

"Mrs. Dewitt….are you okay?" the black officer asked. He noticed she was holding the phone and took it from her. "Hello."

"H….hello." Kiko's now hoarse voice came through.

"This is Officer Blackwell, are you related to Mrs. Dewitt?"

"No, but she's my best friend. I….was just calling to tell her the news. My fiancée was…..was with him."

"Is there anyway someone can come be with Mrs. Dewitt? She's in pretty bad shape right now."

"Let her know I'm on the next plane there."

"Will do?" he said ending the call and giving Orchid the phone. "There are some formality's you'll need to deal with concerning the police in Jersey. Here's the card of the officer handling the case and here's my card. He'll be able to answer any questions you may have."

Orchid didn't remember how she'd gotten to the couch or even how she'd managed to dial the number of the detective on the card, but came to when she heard his loud voice over the phone.

"This is Detective Moore." he answered.

"Hi, uh…..this is Orchid Dewitt…."

"Ahhhh, Mrs. Dewitt. Let me first start by saying I am sorry for your loss."

"Thank you. It….still hasn't registered yet." she said crying "What…..what happened to my husband?"

"It seems as if he and his friends may have been ambushed. There were quite a few shots fired. There are two others that did not make it as well. You know of a Mr. Keon Davies?"

"Yes, that's his best friend and my best friends'

fiancée. Is he......"

"No. He was shot in the shoulder and in the leg, but was treated and being held in custody."

"In custody....for what?"

"Weapons related charges. He should be fine. I do wanna ask- are you familiar with someone who goes by the name Preme?"

"Preme! Yes, unfortunately I do. Did he do this?"

"It appears so....or at least he spear headed the attack. He was injured as well. Unfortunately, he was mistaken for an innocent bystander and wasn't cuffed. I'm sorry to inform you that he did escape the hospital."

"How could that happen!?" Orchid yelled. "He killed my husband and he gets away!?"

"I understand your anger Mrs. Dewitt. Is there any way you can get here to Jersey....we have some paperwork and your husbands' personal effects. We also need you to formally ID his body."

"I.....I'll be there tomorrow."

"Alright. Again....I'm sorry for your loss."

She dropped the phone and all she could do was cry and scream. She was momentarily interrupted when DJ came down the stairs. She looked into his face, a face that belonged to his father and cried some more. She picked up their son and held him like she'd never hold him again.

"No cry mommy." DJ said wiping away her tears. Orchid's cell started ringing off the hook. She didn't have the want or strength to talk to anyone but knew she needed to. She saw it was D's mom so she answered but was unable to speak.

"Orchid! Baby....talk to me."

"They.....they killed him. Why....why'd they take him from me?!" she screamed.

"I know baby. I never thought….I'd outlive my child." she said crying also. "Listen, I don't want you to be alone. I want you and DJ to come stay with me. I need to be near my sons' family."

"I….have to fly out there tomorrow to ID his……body." she said unable to fight back the next wave of tears. "Mom…..I'm pregnant. What am I gonna do….what am I gonna tell DJ?"

"My God." she said and cried some more. "We'll talk about that tomorrow. I want you to get some rest and give my grandson a kiss for me. I love you guys."

"Love you too."

The next call she made was to her mother, who was beside herself. She started packing a bag while they were still on the phone to go be by her daughter's side. Call after call came in, from his boys, his family and her family in Jersey. She'd just cried herself to sleep with DJ on her chest when the doorbell rang. She got up gingerly and laid DJ down, who'd she'd just told that daddy was in heaven, and went to the door. When she opened the door and saw Kiko's face, she broke down all over again. Kiko put Keona's car seat down and took Orchid in her arms.

"Ma……I am…so sorry." she cried and held her friend. "Come on, let's go sit down." she said struggling to hold her up and carry the baby.

"Why? Why did this have to happen Kiko?"

"I wish I had the answers for you ma….I really do. I do know you have to be strong….DJ needs you….I need you."

"Where do I go from here? How am I supposed to live without him? We have a child…..and another one on the way. How Kiko….."

"You're pregnant?"

"Yeah....I told him right before he got on the plane. Now....he's not here....." she cried some more on her friends shoulder. "I need a drink..." she said getting up and going to the bar to make a drink and grab the blunt she'd been smoking.

"Orchid...should you....."

"Just one....I need something to dull the pain. Oh God....how is Keon?"

"Not good. His injuries aren't serious but he's tore up about D. We heard Preme got away."

"That's what the detective told me. Why Kiko? I never led him on; we're out here away from him and all this bullshit. Why?"

"I wish I had the answers for you ma....I really do."

After putting the babies to bed, Kiko helped Orchid to the bed and laid there with her until she fell asleep. When she did, she cried some more. Not only was someone who was like a brother to her gone but her man was facing up to twelve years in prison. Life had definitely taken a turn for the worse.

Kiko finally fell asleep and was awaken shortly afterward by the doorbell. She let Theresa in and greeted her with a long hug.

"How are you doing Kiko?"

"As well as to be expected. It's Orchid I'm worried about. She hasn't eaten anything since I've been here. All she's doing is crying.......and she's pregnant."

"What? She didn't tell me."

"She just found out yesterday."

"My poor baby. Where is she?"

"She's finally sleeping. I'm gonna get her up soon, our flight to Jersey is at noon."

"I can't believe this happened. That no good ass ex of hers took away the person she loved the most since it wasn't him. If I see his ass, I might bust a cap."

"The feeling is mutual."

Theresa and Kiko went into the kitchen to make breakfast and tended to the kids while Orchid still slept. When she did come down into the kitchen, her mom rushed to her daughters' side. She held her as she cried.

"Mom…..he's gone."

"I know baby…..I know, and I'm so sorry for it. How you feeling?"

"Like I lost my husband."

"Come on over here and sit down, I want you to eat something. You need to keep your strength up."

"I'm not hungry mom."

"I know but just take a few bites."

Not having the energy to argue with her mother she did as she was told. After breakfast, they all dressed and left to catch their flight.

As soon as they landed, they stopped at Orchid and D's home to leave the kids with Kiko's sister and went to see Detective Moore. As soon as she mentioned her name she was ushered back to his office. *"Damn she fine!"* the detective thought to himself.

"Mrs. Dewitt, thank you for coming. Again, I'm sorry for your loss."

"Thank you. So…is there any news?"

"Still nothing…..but we do have some things to discuss…in private."

"It's okay. This is my mother and best friend; you can speak freely in front of them."

"Okay. Well, the cause of death was a gunshot in

the back that pierced his heart…." he started.
Orchid grabbed the trash can and buried her face in
it before she began puking and crying. Her mom
rubbed her back; trying to console her while the
detective spoke.

"I'm sorry….."

"Just please….I wanna do this so I can get back to
my son."

"Alright. Well, if you'll follow me, we'll go
downstairs to ID and I'll get you his belongings."
They followed Detective Moore down the dimly lit
hallway to the morgue. Just seeing the words
written on the door made Orchid sick again. She
gathered herself, grabbed bottled water, and
continued on. When they wheeled the table holding
D's body over to her, her legs got weak. When they
pulled the sheet off of his handsome face, she lost it.
It took her mother and Kiko to hold her. Screaming
and crying uncontrollably, she had Kiko confirm
him before having D rolled away. Theresa had her
sitting in a chair holding her when she was
approached with his belongings. The detective
emptied the bag and went over the items that fell
out.

"One set of Mercedes car keys…..five hundred in
cash…..a Rolex….platinum and diamond wedding
band…" which Orchid took from him and placed on
her thumb. "…..and in his jacket pocket, one pink
diamond necklace. We do have to keep the articles
of clothing he was wearing."

"Is there anything she needs to do?" Theresa asked
anxious to get her out of the building.

"There's just some forms that need to be signed and
then we can release his body to the funeral home of
your choosing."

Chapter 12

Although Theresa insisted on her going home to lie down, she wanted to go to the county jail to see Keon. She and Kiko registered to see him and waited their turn to go in. As soon as Keon laid eyes on Orchid, he rushed to her, and pulled her into a tight hug.

"Ma......I am so sorry. If there's anything I could've....."

"Keon, I don't blame you. You did everything you could, you even took two bullets. I just want to know what his last moments were like....what did he say, do."

"He was excited about having another baby...said you held out on him long enough. We went and picked up a necklace he bought you before we........ His last words were to tell you that he loved you; you and his son were his whole world. He also said to be strong and then he....." he stopped as the tears slid down his face. "What up with you ma...how's my princess?" he said trying to change the subject not wanting to cry.

"She good, she's with her auntie right now. How you feeling?"

"I'm not worried about that shit. The only pain I'm feeling right now is because my best friend....my mans is gone." he said getting upset again.

"Orchid....there's some things I need to say to you but I can't say it here. Just know that any and everything I can do to find that pussy ass mother fucker....I'm doing it."

"I appreciate that K....but I need you to worry about getting well and coming back home to your family. We all need you...."

"I know…but in the meantime, I know my baby will hold you down. So uh…..when's the service?" he asked becoming sad and enraged all over again.

"We're going to the funeral parlor to make arrangements. I wanted to come see you first." Orchid said dabbing her eyes.

"I appreciate that O. Kiko, ya'll good? I'mma have my mans' come past to drop off some money and shit. Orchid, you good?"

"You know that man made sure I was straight. I need to go to the ladies room, Kiko I'll meet you outside. Keon…..I love you. Keep your head up." Orchid said and hugged him.

"Don't worry about me….I'm worried about you and DJ. I know you're a strong woman O……continue to be strong. How is my lil man anyway?"

"Big and into everything. He doesn't really understand what's going on but what two year old does. He's excited about having a lil brother or sister." she said and tried to crack a smile.

"Ahhh……" Keon said and dropped his head. "I'm sorry, I forgot. Shit! I wish it was me instead of him….leaving you like this."

"Don't say that." Kiko said with tears in her eyes.

"Don't take it like that ma. I love you and I'm glad that I am here but……..I'm sorry I upset you." he hugged Kiko.

"I didn't mean to upset you all over again. Keon, I'll be in touch. Kiko, I'll be outside."

On unsteady legs, Orchid, D's mom, Theresa and Kiko went into the funeral home to make arrangements for D's burial. Orchid figured since Jersey is where all his family and friends are, that's where he should be buried. During the conversation with the funeral director, Orchid had to grab a trash can and puke. She excused herself to the ladies room and returned to finish so she could leave. Being in the funeral home was making her light headed.

As soon as she stepped foot outside in the fresh air, a flash of heat came over her and she hit the ground.

"Oh my God! Call an ambulance!" Theresa yelled, handing Debbie Lil D and dropping to her knees. "Come on baby….don't do this to me." Theresa cried and pleaded.

Orchid was out for two days before she opened her eyes. When she did awaken, she felt slightly refreshed in her depressed state. She turned her head to the side and saw her mother sleep on the couch with Lil D on her chest.

"Mom" she said softly causing Theresa to stir.

"Oh, thank the Lord." she said getting up and putting Lil D on the couch. "How you feeling?" she said kissing her forehead and holding her hand.

"A lil better. I lost my baby……didn't I?"

"I'm……I'm sorry baby." Theresa said shedding a tear. "They say it was the stress. I am so sorry this happened to you." she cried.

"Mom……it's okay. Not to sound heartless but I think this may have been a blessing in disguise. I don't even know how I'm gonna raise one of D's kids without him, let alone two. I'm gonna have to look into my baby's face…..everyday …and see his father's face. Do you know how that makes me feel? My heart breaks a lil more each and every time."

"Listen to me…." she said taking her chin and

pointing her eyes towards hers. "…..you can do this. I know things are bad, your heart is broken. My hearts breaks for you and my grand baby. You are a strong beautiful black woman. You're a great mom, wife…..and daughter. D knew that. He loved you and DJ. He would not want you to live your life in misery."

"Mom, I know but…."

"No but's Orchid. Don't you give up on life because D's ended. That would mean the person that did this has won. You be the best woman and mother you can be…..you owe it to yourself…..you owe it to DJ and to D. It'll take time to get to the point where you can appreciate what I'm saying. Take that time to mourn….do what you need to…….but don't give up."

Orchid sat through D's service in a coma like state. At times she didn't realize she was crying until she heard herself sobbing. Her mom, Kiko, and Keon sat at her and DJ's side, giving them all the support they needed. She was also overwhelmed by the love D was being shown. His mother's church was very sizeable but yet, there was standing room only. The service went on longer than planned because of all of the guests that wanted to get up and speak on D. To everyone's shock and surprise, Orchid got up with the help of Kiko while her mother held DJ. Orchid approached the podium and received thunderous applause. She heard faint…"take your times" and "be strong." being shouted from the audience.

"I uh…..want to first take the time to thank all of ya'll for coming and paying your respects to D. Although some may not approve to everything he did in his life, no one can argue that he was a great and loving man." she paused shedding a few tears. "This man…..was my life. Where I go from here without him, I don't know. I do know that I have a piece of him with me and I see that every day I look into our sons face. I just wanna urge any and every one….if you know anything…..please let someone know. D can't be brought back…..but the person responsible being brought to justice would give me and the people who loved him most some closure. Thank you all for your love and support. Thank you." she said and carefully walked down the stairs.

After the graveside service, Theresa and Kiko had to practically pry her from D's grave. She reluctantly went with them after tossing red roses on top of his coffin, shedding tears for him and their child that was lost.

Orchid was thankful she had her mother and especially Kiko by her side. Staying in her seat in the dining hall, Kiko and her mom walked around greeting and thanking her guests. Kiko knew all of D's crew from being with Keon so, she interacted with them on her behalf.

"Yo Kiko….Orchid gonna be alright?" Davon, one of D's longtime friends asked.

"She will be….it's gonna take time." she said and pulled him to the side. "She doesn't talk about it so keep this too yourself. She was pregnant….and told D the day he was killed. With all the stress, she lost the baby too." she said in a hushed tone.

"Fuck!" he exclaimed, truly hurt and pissed.

"Yo….that nigga really gonna fucking pay. I'm not gonna say anything to her about this but I'm gonna go holla at her."

"She'd like that."

After spending some time with DJ and putting him to bed, Orchid took a shower, put on one of D's t-shirts and curled up in the bed. All she could do was cry as she laid on his side of their old bed. Her mom tried to get her to eat but was unsuccessful, so she gave it a rest for a while.

"Knock Knock." Kiko stuck her head through the door."

"Hey." Orchid said weakly.

"You feel like some company?"

"Sure....why not." she said as she watched Kiko climb on the bed and produce a blunt. "I figured you could use a lil herbal stimulation."

"I could use some of that. Where's my god daughter?"

"She's knocked out in the guest room and your mom is downstairs getting her drink on.....worrying about you."

"Tell her I'm okay.....or at least I will be. It just.......hurts so bad." she said wiping away tears.

"I can't even begin to imagine what you're feeling right now ma. I know you're hurting and so are the rest of us. I loved D, your mom loved D and Keon......he loves D. I couldn't even talk to him this morning he was so upset and I was getting more upset listening to him."

"With everything.....I didn't even think about Keon. If he calls again, let me talk to him."

"I will." Kiko said handing her a blunt.

"So........what are you gonna do know?" she asked with tears in her eyes. She knew that was a loaded question and was afraid of what her answer may be.

"I honestly don't know Kiko. If you asked me two weeks ago, I could give you an answer and it wouldn't include burying my husband. Now......I have no clue."

"Are you sticking around Jersey for a while? I could

keep a closer eye on your ass."

"I don't know…..it's just… I just know I'm not ready to be alone, so I guess I'll be here for a while."

"Glad to hear it. You know I love you…..so that means me being hard on you when you won't welcome it. I'm gonna help you through this O…just know that anything I say or do will be done outta love."

"I know…..and I love you too. Right now, I need that…..I need you."

"I'm here for whatever you need."

For the next two weeks, Orchid lived in her pajamas. She was good about making sure Lil D was taken care of, she had to……he was her reason for living. Her life had taken a tragic turn for the worse and how she would recover and move on…….the answer had yet to come to her.

She and Lil D were cuddled on the couch watching the Lion King enjoying some quality time. He was the light in her life. Although every time she looked at him, it pained her to see his father's face…but it also brought her joy. She had a piece of D to hold on to and for that she was grateful.

"What mommy?" Lil D, now almost 3 said.

"I love you my lil man."

"Love mommy too. Kiss!" he said and puckered his adorable lips.

"I think we are gonna go on a nice lil trip…..to a place where the waters are crystal blue and me and your daddy made the most beautiful love."

"Daddy sleeping."

"Yes…..he's sleeping."

By the following week, without any

warning…Lil D and Orchid were relaxing in their house in Barbados. When Orchid walked into the house she felt a wave of love and shed tears of pain and joy at the memories they'd made there. She picked Lil D up and climbed the stairs to show him his bedroom and the rest of the house. Not really interested in anything else but the toys in his room, D left out the master bedroom to play. Orchid stood in the middle of the bedroom taking in her surroundings….when she noticed a frame of some sort with a sheet over it. She pulled it back and shed tears. It was a picture D just had to have taken after seeing Will Smith's video "Just the Two of Us". Orchid laid on the chaise lounge naked, covering her breasts and D listening to her belly with a hand on it. The picture brought both smiles and tears. She kicked off her shoes picked up the painting and mounted it over their bed and smiled. She laid on the bed, holding his pillow just reminiscing.

"Daddy!" Lil D pointed at the picture.

"Yes." Orchid said and picked him up. "And that's you in my belly right here." she said pointing.

"Oh! Can we eat mommy?"

"Okay…..let's go get something to eat." she said leaving out the bedroom as her cell rang. "Hello."

"Bitch! What is wrong with you!" Kiko yelled into the phone. "You up and leave the country without saying a word! What is wrong with you?"

"I'm sorry Kiko. I needed to be here and I knew you'd try to talk me out of it."

"You damn right! You at least could've let me come with you for a lil while. I was worried." Kiko said crying.

"Don't cry Kiko. I'm sorry, you're right….I

should've told you. But we're fine."

"I'm not. At least let me come out there for a lil while to be with you."

"Kiko……"

"Don't Kiko me…..wsup?"

"Fine…..I guess we could use the company. When you wanna come?"

"Asap! You just leave your scared, worried best friend out here without a clue."

"I'm sorry ma….you know I'd never abandon you and my god child."

"I know. I'm gonna find a flight like yesterday….and please call your mom."

"I'll call her when I get off the phone with you."

"You also need to call Fedex. I stopped at the house and they were there with a delivery from the insurance company. You might wanna handle that."

"I'll give them a call in the morning."

"Alright. Is there anything you need from the house? Is Lil D okay?"

"He's fine. I've hardly seen him since he's discovered his new room."

"I miss him…..I miss ya'll. Let me get on this flight and I'll call you back. Call you mother O." Kiko said sternly.

"As soon as you get off my damn phone, I will."

Theresa chewed Orchid a new asshole. After being relieved of her worries, she understood that Orchid needed to be where she felt close to D…..to heal. After chatting a few minutes, they exchanged "I love you's" and hung up. She dabbed at the tears in her eyes and went upstairs to check on D. Sitting in front of the flat screen hypnotized by Nick, she couldn't get no rap. She giggled and left him alone.

"Love you." he said not looking away from the screen.

"Love you too baby."

Kiko rushed into Orchids' arms like she hadn't seen her in years. Little did she know that would soon be the case. They embraced each other and cried for a few minutes before sitting down to talk, while the baby was napping.

"You look good heifer. I guess the island sun agrees with you." Kiko smiled.

"I love it here…..and this house holds a lot of good, important memories. I think it helps…me being here. But look at you."

"Girl, Please. I look like shit."

"So, how's Keon?"

"He's doing okay. It looks like he may have some time shaved off his sentence due to "new evidence that was not available at trial"" she quoted. "Such bullshit!"

"Sounds like it. Well that's good news. How long will he have?"

"Looks like five years."

"That's better than ten to twelve……or forever." Orchid said with a hint of sadness.

"Aww ma." she said placing her arm around Orchid.

"It's okay. I have my moments but I'm getting there. They say acceptance is the first step, then anger….which I've dealt with. Now, I'm just waiting for the rest of my life to begin."

"Honey…..it already has. You are a strong beautiful black woman and mother. You can and will get through this and be sitting on top of the world when it's all said and done. Trust me."

"Thank you….that means a lot."

"Your welcome. So…..I'm hungry and I smell it. What's for dinner?"

"Greedy. We better go wake up your god son. His particular ass has a fit if I eat dinner without him. He is his father's child. Oh….what until you see what I found in the bedroom when I got here. I'll show it to you before we wake up my lil monster."

Kiko was speechless when she saw the oversized mural over the bed. It was beautiful. "O….that is beautiful. This is indeed a sign that D is and always will be watching over you and his son."

"You are right…"

"Ma!" Lil D started yelling from his room.

"Up…there's your god son paging now. Go in there in get his ass." Orchid said laughing.

"Ki!" D yelled with his little face all lit up.

"Hi Aunties baby." Kiko picked him up and hugged him tightly with tears in her eyes.

"Getting big isn't he?" Orchid asked.

"Big is not the word. Awwww, I miss you so much."

"Miss you." he said and kissed her. "Mommy, I'm hungry."

"Let's go eat, Aunt Kiko is hungry anyway."

Kiko stayed with them in the islands for almost a month before heading back home. Since Keon insisted she stay home, she had the time but needed to get back to see to some of his personal affairs. They shed tears as they embraced each other at the airport before she got on her flight.

"So….when are you coming back?"

"Kiko…..I honestly don't know. When I do, you

will be the first to know ma."

"I won't press." she hugged her again. "I'll call you when I get home. I love you ma."

"I love you too."

Chapter 13

Five Years Later

Orchid laid in the warm sand while a now seven year-old Lil D buried her in the sand. She giggled when he placed two sea shells over where her breasts were before finishing off his masterpiece. He stood up and smiled at his handy work.

"Mom….you look funny." D laughed.

"You laughing at me….wait until I get outta here." she pretended to be struggling to move.

"You can't." he laughed again. "Hey Mr. Jean!" D greeted a neighbor Orchid had become friends with. "Can you take a picture of me and mom?"

"Sure." he said taking the camera from D's hands. "Nice shells." he said and laughed taking the picture.

"Same thing I said." she laughed. "Can you help me out now, I have to pee." she said and laughed causing D to giggle.

"I guess so." he kissed Orchid and started digging her out.

"I came over to see if you and lil man wanna come over later. I'm letting my sister have my niece's birthday party at the house."

"Can we mom?"

"Sure. What time shall we be there?"

"Four o'clock."

"Well, we better get home and clean up if we're gonna be on time."

"Cool!"

Orchid sat at her computer smoking a blunt while she waited for Kiko to pick up her end of the video chat. She hadn't held her god daughter in the longest but didn't miss out on a thing. She missed her other home, her friends and her family but didn't know if she was ready to move back into the house she shared with D. Speaking with Kiko on the regular was a constant reminder of what her fear was causing her to miss out on.

"Who's this video chatting with my wife?!"

"Oh my God! Keon....when did you get home?!" she yelled excitedly.

"Late last night. We were just gonna call you. How you been? You looking good."

"Thank you. I'm great. I've come a long way with the help of my best friend over there."

"I'm glad to hear that. Yo...they giving me a big welcome home party, I want you there."

"When is it?"

"Two weeks. I wanna keep it on the low; spend time with my family before I announce my arrival."

"I heard that. I don't know if I'll make it though."

"We family right?"

"You know we are....why?"

"Cause I'm gonna give you some tough love. Stop with the scared bullshit O. D was the happiest he's ever been with you. He was taken too soon, but he always said if he was to die all he wanted was for you to be happy. I know you may be okay but you ain't happy out there with just lil D. Stop the bullshit and come home. We miss you and need to see you....not you on a computer screen."

"Keon...."

"Don't Keon me. I'm not gonna jump on your case too bad but you think about it. Where's my nephew? Does he look like his big head daddy?"

"I'll let you see for yourself. D......come say hi to your uncle Keon." Orchid yelled.

"Uncle Keon...I thought he was in college?"

"He's finished...come here." she put him on her lap.

"Hey uncle Keon."

"Hey Lil man....how you doin'?"

"Good. We going to a birthday party. When are you visiting?"

"Hopefully your mom will bring you to visit us....maybe even move back here where your family is."

"Oh mom can we?! I wanna see my cousins."

"We'll see. Go finish getting dressed."

"Okay. Bye Uncle Keon."

"Aiight D. Yo......." he paused getting choked up. "I was not prepared for that. It's like looking at the nigga all over again."

"I know. That's my heart. D definitely left a part of him with me when we made that boy. He's smart as hell and definitely has his fathers' temperament."

"I can't wait to see him. I'mma let you talk to your girl but think about what I said. Oh by the way, just in case this is part of the reason....they got Preme. He's been in prison for a couple months."

"W...what?!"

"They got him ma. And that nigga got his before he went in. I got you."

"Keon......I....I don't know what to say."

"Say you'll come home. Time to start the next chapter. I love you....holla at you soon."

All night long Orchid tossed and turned. Her mind was going a mile a minute and Keon's forceful suggestion still burned in her head. Preme was in jail, she accepted D's passing and was living a happy life for her and her son. D wouldn't want her to live the rest of her life mourning him, so......she flipped a coin and it landed on home.

Orchid called an interior decorator and had her make a few changes to the home she once shared with D. She also sent pictures of D's room in Barbados, which he loved, to model his room the same. Without letting Kiko and Keon know a thing, she closed up their home in Barbados, said good bye to the friends she'd made and boarded a plane with her son. They were going home.

They walked through the door of the house and she was emotional. She didn't cry this time, instead, she wore a smile. She went up to their old bed room and hung the mural she'd brought from the house in Barbados before checking out the changes to the rest of the house. She had to do a happy dance....she was home and missed it more than she allowed herself to realize.

"Mommy....is this our house too! I see pictures of dad here."

"Yes, this is our house too. You like your room?"

"Yup. It's like my other room...only better."

"Good. We're gonna change clothes and go visit Keona, Aunt Kiko and uncle Keon. But first we have to go to the bank and then the mall."

"Can I get a new toy?"

"Yeah but only if you can be changed and ready in ten minutes."

"Okay!" he said and took off out the door.

Lil D came racing into the kitchen eight minutes later with one shoe untied and out of breath.

"Please tie your shoe before you hurt yourself."

"Mom, we don't have a car how we getting there?"

"We have more than one car thank you. See?" She said turning on the garage light. "Which one do you want to ride in?"

"The white one!" he yelled.

"That car will belong to you one day. That was your daddy's favorite car. When you're old enough to drive it…it's yours."

"Really!?"

"Yup. So how about we drive the other white one?"

"Yeah, I like trucks."

After a brief stop at the bank and then the mall to pick up a few things for Keona, Keon, D and Kiko they headed over to their house.

Inside the elaborate home Kiko thought she was seeing things when she saw Orchid's old truck pull up into the driveway. When she saw her best friend and god son get out her mouth dropped open.

"What's wrong ma?" Keon asked hugging her from behind.

"What did you say to Orchid?"

"Nothing much….just gave it to her straight. Why wsup?"

"Wsup is you accomplished in one phone call what I've been trying to do for years. Look." she pointed to her and D grabbing bags out the car.

"Oh shit! Look at my lil dude. So, you gonna let'em in or keep looking at them from the window."

"I'm going smart ass."

"Am I dreaming or what?" she screamed from the door.

"Aunt Kiko!" D yelled running into her arms.

"Hey Doo!" she called him by his nickname and kissed him. "I missed you."

"I missed you too. Where's Keona?"

"She's in her room. I want you to say hello to Uncle Keon first though."

"Ok…where he at?"

"Where is he?" Orchid corrected him.

"Yeah…."

"I'm right here lil man. Come show me some love."

It touched Orchid's heart seeing them interact with each other. The sight alone was confirmation that she made the right decision. No one could ever replace his father, but Keon was the next best thing.

"You better getter your model looking ass over here and give your brother some love." Keon stood and opened his free arm. "You better not ever stay away for five years ever again. We will through down. Got me?"

"I got you." she answered and smiled. "Damn what you been eating up in there. You all big and buff."

"Isn't he. I'm loving it." Kiko beamed.

"Pervert." Orchid laughed. "Let us go see Ms. Keona before this one has a fit." Orchid said taking D's hand and climbing the stairs.

"You look like a kid on Christmas morning." Keon teased Kiko.

"My missing link is home…..both of them." she said and kissed him.

"I missed you so much ma."

"I missed you too….more than you'll ever know."

"Well, I'm here now and I got a lot of catching up to do with you and Keona. Now I have to add Orchid and my lil man in the mix. Damn! I still miss my nigga. His seed…..man, that's him all over again."

"It's like D in a tiny body."

"For real. I know I'mma have to put some niggas on notice. No disrespect but your girl is on some tropical looking shit and niggas will try to holla. Ain't nobody fucking my fam over."

"Yes Daddy. You turn me on when you get all…….alpha male." she said grabbing his dick.

"Damn ma!" he said and let out a light moan. "As much as I wanna bend you over and get some of my pussy, we got company. Best believe daddy gonna have you climbing the walls later though." he said kissing her neck.

"We can clear the house now." she said and giggled.

"Be easy ma. Let's round up our lil posse and go out to dinner. We celebrating two home comings."

Orchid and Lil D practically lived at Keon and Kiko's house. It was like old times and D's presence was sorely missed. Instead of sadness, they smiled and laughed at memories of D. He would always be with them but it was past time to move on. The only thing left to do was to visit D's grave, something Orchid has yet to have done since she returned.

She knelt down and brushed the leaves off of his head stone and placed the flowers there. She looked at the picture of his smiling face on the concrete and smiled at his handsome face.

"I know it took me a long time to get here babe. I needed that time…..in order to keep going. You leaving me was the hardest thing to deal with. I will always love and keep you with me. I do know it's time to move on and I will always keep you and D in mind with every decision I make. I wish you could see him. He's so big and he looks just like you…..acts like you too. I make sure he knows who you are and he loves you so much. I just want to be happy baby and I know now you want that too. I will love you forever D." she said and stood.

"I will too." Keon said from behind her.

"Hey….you scared me."

"My bad. You okay?"

"I'm good…..I can finally say that. You?"

"Yeah. I just haven't been here yet. I guess we were thinking the same thing huh? Kiko showed me some pictures. You put him away nice."

"Thank you but your wife is a big part of that. I was so out of it K. She took a hold of the reigns and personally made sure everything was right….even me. I'll never be able to repay her for that."

"She feels the same about you. Hold up, I just wanna put this on his grave." Keon said pulling out the replica of a bullet.

"What is that?"

"It's a mold of the bullet I had specially made….the bullet that's gonna end Preme's life."

"Keon….I know you loved D but your family needs you. Don't do anything that will take you away from them. I don't want Kiko to ever have to go through what I did."

"I won't let that happen….trust. Come on, let's go grab one of those milkshakes that D used to always bring you home."

"You remember that huh?"

"I remember everything."

They got caught up over milkshakes and a blunt. They talked about D, how close she came to losing it after he and the baby were gone and the long road to recovery for her. He even opened up about the night D was murdered and his time in prison. The conversation was very cleansing, she felt lighter and closer to Keon. She truly loved her family. Then he had to embarrass her. "So....when you plan on dating again? Kiko told me you've been on lockdown this whole time."

"I'm gonna bust her ass!" she yelled. "You just gonna embarrass me like that?"

"My bad. Hey, you like my lil sister....I need to know these things. You know whoever it is gots to have my stamp of approval."

"Oh I know that all too well. Actually, I haven't given it much thought. I mean....I know it's time, but what if I meet someone and I can't stop comparing him to D."

"I know D is who you want, but he's gone. I feel like you've accepted that and moved on....so stop being scared. You know we got you."

"I know ya'll do."

"Good. Now I want you to do something for me."

"What's up?"

"We did the ceremony thing while I was in prison but I want more for ma. She always had this thing about...."

"A wedding on the beach in June." they said in unison.

"You know her too well." he laughed. "I wanna hook something up. I figure its March, we can hook something up for June."

"I would love to help....only if you let me help pay for it."

"Get the fuck outta here! I got this. Just keep her ass out the business."

"I got this. We better get back to the house before D starts calling me."

"What?! He be on you like that?"

"Every since he got his cell and learned my number he calls me all the time."

"Yeah, ya'll done started some shit. Now Keona wants a phone."

"Glad to know, now I'll get her one."

"Here we go with the bullshit."

Chapter 14

Orchid was excited about Keon's party that night. It's been way too long since the last time she and her girl cut up at a club. Something she missed a lot. She was dancing in the closet with her towel on looking for an outfit.

"Go mommy.....go mommy!" Lil D danced with her.

"Hey Doo....what's up?"

"Do I have to go to Aunt Val's? I wanna play with Keona."

"Keona is going over there with you. I want you to finish packing your bag because we have to pick her up."

"Okay!" he perked and ran off.

Orchid decided on a pair of fitted Seven jeans, bustier, matching half jacket, red Loubotins and a red Hermes purse. She checked her make up, sprayed some Issey Miake, grabbed Keon's gift and left out her room.

"You ready Doo?"

"Yup. You look pretty mommy."

"Thank you. Let's go....mama's ready to party!"

When Orchid got back to Kiko and Keon's house the driveway was filled and there were cars parked on the street. All of Keon's entourage were leaving from the house in limos. She found a spot, grabbed the gift, and strutted up to the house.

"Yo Keon.....who the fuck is that?!" his man's Khalil from Manhattan asked.

"That's my lil sis....D's widow."

"Are you serious? How she doin'....she aiight?" he asked outta respect for D.

"She good man.....can't you tell. What it do girl?"

he hugged her when she walked into the living room.

"Hey Big Head. I got you a lil something." she said handing him a box and stood as he opened it.

"Is this.......?"

"I know much you loved it and tried to get D for it, so I wanted you to have it."

"Awww man. Nah, give it to Lil D."

"Keon....Lil D has more than enough of his father's things that he will get when he's old enough. This one is special to you so I want you to have it. Don't argue with me, I'll slap the shit outta you." she laughed.

"I don't want no problems. Love you sis." he said and hugged her.

"You're welcome....love you too. Now where my girl?"

"Stop being rude....let me introduce you to some people. This right here is my man Khalil........."

Keon took her around the room making introductions before he released her. Grateful to leave the room full of testosterone, she climbed the stairs to the bedroom where Kiko was almost dressed.

"Damn look at you. You make me wanna change." Kiko said and pouted.

"Girl, you look hot! Your husband just got finished introducing me to a hundred niggas, whose names I won't remember at the end of the night. Except for one...."

"Kalil!" they said in unison.

"How you know?" Orchid asked.

"I know my best friend. Besides, he is fine as hell and so your type."

"I didn't know I had a type."

"Bitch, please. So……bam! How do I look?"

"Stunner!" she said and gave her a high five.

"Yo ma! Come on….it don't take that long for you to get dressed." Keon yelled up the stairs.

"We coming now." she yelled back. "You need to holla at him. It's been a long time…..and I know you need some dick."

"I know it's time and I'm looking at things with an open mind. As far as the dick thing…I could use some. In the meantime, I have plenty of hardware to keep the cobwebs away." Orchid said and laughed.

"You nasty!" Kiko said and laughed. "So, tell me about that hardware."

After a champagne toast, all in attendance at the house loaded into the limos and headed to the club. Keon, Kiko, Orchid, Khalil and the few others in their stretch Hummer passed a couple L's around while the limos behind them unloaded. Kiko and Orchid had a blunt of their own to share and were cutting up and the night hadn't started yet.

"I see you over there moving in your seat ma. Can you move like that on the dance floor?" Khalil asked Orchid.

"Uh oh….sounds like a challenge." Kiko yelled souping her girl up.

"Boy…..you don't want to see me on the dance floor. I don't do the same ole two step." she said and laughed as she took the blunt from Kiko.

"Wow….beauty and a slick mouth. I like it but I'll have to see if you can back that up." Khalil said and smiled revealing 32 perfectly white teeth.

"I guess we'll have to see then."

"Uh oh…it's on! You better watch yourself boy….she's a bad mother……"

"Watch yo mouth." Orchid and Kiko said in unison. "Aiight ya'll, let's get this party started!" Keon said opening the door before helping Kiko and Orchid out the car. "Yo….for real, she do the damn thing. If your game ain't tight, shit ain't gonna turn out right." he whispered to Khalil.

"Oh….my shit stay tight. Come on yo….you the man of the hour!"

Kiko did the damn thing with the decoration and arrangements for the party. Of course there were some haters because VIP was by invitation only. If you didn't have a pass or come in with someone who did, you were just a regular regardless of how much cash you had.

The ladies had two booths of their own. Kiko, Orchid, their friend Saunie and Keon's sisters were at their table. His cousins and niece were at the other booth. Keon made sure the ladies had anything they wanted. Henny Black and Brazilian Kush filled the air. Kiko and Orchid deserved to get it in and enjoy each other, they'd both been through a lot and the night was a celebration….of the past being the past and moving on to a bright future.

"Aiight girl! You know what time it is….I needs to hit the dance floor." Kiko yelled in Orchid's ear. "Heyyy!" she yelled. "Come on Saunie!" she said snatching her out her seat before she had a chance to protest.

As soon as they hit the floor the DJ started spinning old school classic "I just wanna Love Ya" by Jay-Z. They immediately got hyped. Kiko and Orchid danced circles around each other, enjoying themselves like the old days.

"I missed you girl!" Kiko yelled and hugged her.

"I missed you….I love you Kiko."

"I love you too."

Keon stood overhead admiring his wife and his brother from another mothers' widow. He was happy seeing them happy and together again. He was also thinking about the things he planned on doing to her beautiful body.

"What up big man? Scoping things out?" Khalil walked up, giving him dap.

"Oh, we good. Just admiring my ladies down there doing they thing."

"Oh yeah…..ma owes me a dance."

"Oh you gonna get one too." Keon laughed. "You my man and all….the closest to me besides D. So I'm gonna tell you up front. If you gonna holla at her, be straight up…..no bullshit. She's been through more than enough."

"You know I ain't on no busta shit K. If I come at her, it'll be correct."

"If…..who you kidding nigga. I know her personally so I know you gonna holla. She's a good girl…..add beautiful and smart. You got the total package."

"I feel you. I'm gonna go get this dance….I'll holla."

"I'm coming with you….get my grind on."

They worked their way through the crowd giving dap and showing love until they got over to the ladies. Keon wasted no time grinding against Kiko's ass to "Murder She Wrote," by Chaka Demus and Plies.

"So…..you up for that challenge now or what?" Khalil asked and smirked.

"Bring it boo." Orchid said and started gyrating.

By the second song, Orchid had Khalil hypnotized

by her body movements and he was sweating. He kept up his end, but she put him to shame on the dance floor. Once the DJ started spinning Baltimore Club, all he could do is grab her waist and hold on for dear life.

Although a little startling feeling a man's hands on her hips after so long, Orchid was enjoying Khalil's touch. It felt good to have her body touching another hard body. She turned around and dabbed his head with a napkin.

"You can say Uncle or I can keep going." she said and laughed.

"I ain't saying uncle but you won......you won ma."

"I'll take that, thank you."

"Aiight. Let me get you a victory drink."

"Aiight."

He took her hand and they made their way through the crowd back up to VIP. He sat in her booth since their booth was occupied so he could spend a lil time getting to know her better.

"So, what's your pleasure?" he asked smiling at her.

"I will have some Henny Black to chase this blunt." she said and laughed.

"I like a woman who knows what she wants."

"I like a man that can recognize I'm a woman who knows what I want. So Khalil right? Where are you from again?"

"I'm from Manhattan. I lived here in Jersey the first few years of my life but after my parents split up we moved. Keon actually would've been my step brother had our parents gotten married. We were close and stayed that way despite their drama."

"That's nice. I don't know if I remember hearing about you."

"That's understandable. I have heard about you. I was sorry to hear about D's passing....sorry for your loss."

"Thank you. It's taken me a while but I've dealt with his passing and now after picking up the pieces, it's time to move onward and upward."

"I'm glad you're happy. You have kids right?"

"One...Lil D. He's almost eight now and acts like he's my father."

"He's doing his job as man of the house. That's wsup."

"I'm glad you see it that way. So, how about you....any kids?"

"I have a daughter, she's five. Lives in Georgia with her mother. I see her on holidays and in the summer."

"That's nice. A daughter huh? Now you really have to be careful to treat your woman the way you want a man to treat your daughter."

"I would.....if I had a woman. I'm just really getting settled in back here and I haven't really met any real woman up until tonight." he said and smiled.

'Is that a compliment?" she said and smiled.

"I would hope so." he laughed.

They partied the rest of the night. Champagne and Henny was flowing like water. Orchid and Khalil danced and talked off and on the remainder of the night....until all the Henny she'd consumed kicked in.

She, Kiko and Saunie were on their way back up to the VIP section when they ran into Shell and her crew of skanks. Orchid immediately sobered up and was breathing fire.

"O.....be easy." Saunie said touching her arm.

"Oh I'm good. It's Keon's party so I'm not gonna set it off….but if the bitch wanna get stupid, I will beat dat ass!"

"Orchid! Is that you? Heyyyyy!" she said and reached to hug her. "When you get back?"

"About a week ago."

"You should've told me, we could've had lunch. How long you in town for?"

"I'm not sure yet. D and I are just visiting right now."

"How is my lil cousin?"

"He's fine."

"You know my mom moved right?"

"I've been to the house a few times."

"She ain't tell me."

"That's because she knows I'm not fucking with you like that. It was nice seeing you, but I have a bottle with my name on it."

"It's like that? We family."

"Did you think about that when you were starting shit with the man that killed my husband? No….so don't talk that shit to me now."

"I'm a different person now….that was my bad."

"Yeah…..well actions speak louder than words."

"You ready O?" Kiko asked ready to pop off.

"We ain't done talking." Shell snapped.

"I'm gonna give you a pass because I don't wanna fuck up my husbands' party but let me say this. I am not the same bitch I used to be, I will fuck your world up every chance I get. You fuck with me, O or anyone associated with me and it's a wrap for your ass. Believe that! We out."

Despite their run in with Shell they had a ball. After thanking his guests for coming out and popping a couple more bottles, they piled up in their limos and went to their hotel. After getting checked in, showered and changed, they chilled in Keon and Kiko's two bedroom suite smoking and playing cards. Saunie and Orchid were put off the table so they sat in the living room with Khalil and Keon's cousin Donte smoking an L.

"I see you can get your party on ma." Khalil said sitting next to Orchid.

"When I want to. I can't go hard like I used to but I can hang with the big dogs a lil something."

"I see. So....you think we can exchange math, go out sometime?"

"I think we can do that. I don't fuck on the first date though." she said with a straight face causing Khalil to choke on the smoke he held in.

"Wow....she wild as hell!" Donte said.

"Gimme some!" Saunie said giving Orchid dap.

"You tryna kill a nigga, shit!" he said still laughing.

"Ma, on the real....if I just wanted pussy I can get that. I'm trying to wine, dine, then sixty nine!"

"What?!" it was her turn to choke. "Oh, okay.......touche."

"Un huh. You're number will do for now....we'll talk about that other stuff later if need be."

"Cocky nigga." she said and laughed.

"Yo Keon.....why you introduce me to this crazy ass girl!" Khalil yelled laughing.

"Hey....proceed with caution my nigga! Young buck!" Keon said and laughed.

"Ya'll better stop talking about me like I'm not in the room. Forget ya'll and good night."

"Where your ass think you going?" Kiko asked.

"I'm taking my ass to bed. I'm fucked up, tired.......and horny." she said looking at Khalil and laughing. "That last part was a joke." she said half kiddingly.

"Don't punk out! These niggas is getting off the table in a minute and I owe you another ass whipping. So sit yo ass down and tutor your partner real quick, cause ya'll got next!" Keon yelled at her.

"I guess he told yo ass!" Kiko laughed.

"Shut up!"

Chapter 15

Over the next few weeks Orchid was busy putting her life back in order and making preparations for Keon and Kiko's wedding and Lil D's birthday in May. Although she was in no way hurting in the financial sense, she wanted to do something. Just sitting at home all day was something she had a hard time adjusting too, so she took a job with a local hospital. For the first time in years Orchid could say that she was happy with life and where she was in it.

Being busy with job hunting, wedding planning and school registration, Orchid didn't have time......make that, didn't make time to call Khalil. The attraction she had towards him was undeniable but she thought maybe it was wrong. After repeated conversations with Kiko and Keon, she decided to finally return his many phone calls.

"What?! I get a call back? Let me sit down." he said jokingly.

"Shut up! I've been crazy busy."

"And scared. It's cool, I understand."

"Not scared.....a lil nervous maybe."

"No need for that. If you stop bullshitting and let me take you out...you'll see I'm the best thing since sliced cheese."

"You think very highly of yourself, don't you?"

"I'm a cocky nigga.....didn't you say that?"

"I guess I did." she laughed.

"So, you gonna stop bullshitting and let me take you out tonight?"

"It just so happens I'm free tonight, so yes. And not because you said I'm scared."

"Uh huh...I know. You wanna give me your

address or you wanna meet?"

"Since Keon says you good peoples, you can pick me up."

"Aiight....be ready by eight."

"Yes sir!"

"Aiight beautiful.....I'll talk to you later."

"Hey mom!" D said hopping into the car and kissing her cheek.

"Hey Doo. How was school?"

"Good. Am I still staying the night with grandma?"

"Yup and Grandma Theresa will be here to see you next weekend."

"Yeah!"

"So, we're gonna go home to pack you a bag and then I'll drop you off. Okay?"

"Yes. Mom....do we have to go back to our other house by the water?"

"Why you ask?"

"I like it here with all my cousins and grandma and Aunt Kiko and Keona. And uncle Keon is the best!"

"Well, I thought we could live in our house here so you can be close to all those people you love."

"Really, can we?!"

"I wouldn't have it any other way."

Orchid was nervous as hell about her date with Khalil. There definitely was an attraction but this was the first time in years she would be next to a man on an intimate level other than D. She rolled a blunt of some weed that Keon left last time he visited and fired it up. She sat on the couch and let the marijuana take effect. She wasn't half way through the blunt and she was so relaxed she'd kicked off her shoes and poured a glass of wine. Returning from the kitchen her doorbell rang.

"Damn! You look good."

"Thank you….you look pretty handsome yourself." Orchid said through a smile. "Come on in for a minute. I was practicing some herbal medicine while I waited for you."

"Oh ok. This is a nice crib….you got good taste."

"Thank you. You want some wine?"

"I'm not a wine drinker. Straight yak is all I drink."

"I do have some of that. You're not a bad driver are you? I don't want to end up wrapped around a pole cause you can't hold your liquor."

"Wow….Keon said you got mad jokes but he underestimated." he said and laughed. "Ma…I'm a professional."

"Aiight. You kill me, I'mma fuck you up."

"You got that."

After another blunt and a drink, Khalil took her to Philadelphia for dinner on the waterfront. Afterwards, they hit up a club that his cousin owned for a few drinks. Khalil was feeling Orchid; she definitely portrayed strong, beautiful, and intelligent at all times. They settled into a booth and Khalil ordered a bottle of Henny and champagne for Orchid before firing up a L.

"So….what's up with you? Tell me more about you beautiful."

"What do you wanna know?"

"What are your intentions with me?" he asked with a smirk.

"You funny as hell!" she laughed.

"I'm serious. I don't want to be led on and you toss me in the trash like an old pair of pantyhose." he said chuckling.

"And I'm the one with the jokes?" Orchid laughed. "Honestly, I have no idea what my intentions are. I think you cool and I'm interested in getting to know you better. As far as leading you on and throwing you away....I don't lead people on. I'm as real as real can get and when I do decide to give myself to you or anyone else....I play for keeps. Which is why I'm very selective of who I get involved with."

"Real talk....okay. So does that mean I've been selected?"

"So far you've made the first cut."

"I'll take that....for now." he said *'I got intentions on winning the whole fucking thing ma. Bet that!"*

Orchid had a good time with Khalil and surprised even herself when she kissed him.....with a little tongue too. After sleeping in and dressing, she picked up Kiko and they went to her Aunt Val's house to pick up Lil D and Keona for lunch. As soon as Kiko got in the car she started with her line of questioning.

"So....did you sleep with him?" she asked excitedly.

"On the first date?! You done lost your damn mind!"

"Shit....as fine as he is, I would've fucked him when he picked me up!" Kiko laughed.

"Listen at you....I'm telling."

"Yeah okay. You gotta admit, he is fine."

"Fine.....that's an understatement. You should see that niggas body...bananas!"

"I thought you didn't sleep with him bitch!"

"I didn't. We were at the club and this dude was all drunk, boasting and shit. Khalil got up and was fucking with him. He took off his shirt and shut shit down."

"Damn! It's like that?"

"Unh huh! Anyway, where's my brother in law?"

"Apartment hunting with Khalil. He's been staying with his man but he said he's a pig, so he getting his own. You don't know how happy that nigga is that ya'll are back. He said he can keep a close eye on you. He's like D's personal guard dog and spokesperson."

"I love him for that. I'm happy to be back too. I missed the hell outta all of you and I'm sorry I shut you out. I wanted to say that."

"I'm not gonna front….I was pissed at you. But Keon made me realize I can't take it personally, that you needed that time. So I understand and I forgive you…….as long as we can go use the house in Barbados for a vacation sometime. We won't sleep in ya'll bed."

"You better not!" Orchid laughed. "I'm okay with everything though. It doesn't mean that I don't miss or love D….I always will. I finally realized I can't live my life in mourning. I had to let go for me, D and our family and POW! Here I is!"

"I'm glad you're happy again and we are back to being two peas in a pod."

"We always were and always will be."

"So…..what you gonna do with all that fineness that is Khalil?"

"I don't know just yet. I guess we'll see how things go. I may have to get me some dick out the deal if nothing else though." Orchid laughed.

"That's what I'm talking 'bout! Gimme some!"

Orchid loved her baby to death but he was a bundle of energy and she needed a break. They both had a long weekend from school and work so Theresa decided to come get Lil D and take him back to Arizona with her for a few days. She, her mom and Lil D had lunch before she kissed them and watched them board their flight. She missed her baby already but knew he was in good hands.

She was singing along with Ledisi's "Pieces of Me" in the car when her check engine light came on. "Damn" she said aloud. She loved her XL7, it's been with her since before she met D, but she decided it was time to put it out the pasture. She drove along popping her fingers until she rode past a car dealership that had the most beautiful Lincoln Aviator on display. That was as good a sign as any that it was time to trade up. She pulled into the parking lot and walked over to the truck. It was a metallic pearled silver color and she was lovin' it. "Beautiful." she heard a voice from behind her say. "Excuse me?"

"Beautiful.....that car. Isn't it?"

"Oh....yes, it is. It caught my eye from the road."

"I think it would be a perfect match....a beautiful car for a beautiful lady." the salesman said with a lil swagger. "I'm Javan Mitchell and you are?"

"Orchid Dewitt." she said extending her hand to shake his but got it kissed instead.

"So...are you interested in trading in....are you interested in the car?"

"Damn straight. This is so me. Does it have TV's and all that in it?"

"This particular car is fully loaded. It's brand new and comes equipped with DVD, TV, navigation, satellite radio....you name it, and it has it. You wanna take it for a spin?"

"Absolutely."

"Let me grab some keys and we'll take it out." Orchid was in love with the car by the time she made it through two lights. Loving her music loud and thumping, she had to crank up the system to see if it knocked….and she was more than happy. She'd already decided before they got back to the dealership that she was taking the truck home with her.

"So….you wanna go inside and run some figures…..for the car and for me?" Javan said and smiled.

"Ummm….I guess we can do that." she said and smiled. He was damn attractive even though light skinned men weren't really her thing.

"Follow me." Javan said. He wanted to make the sale, but he was more interested in Orchid. He insisted to a co-worker that he would take her, since he assumed her credit was gonna be fucked and had no money….he was fine with it. "I'll just need the keys to the car outside so we can have a look at it while we run some figures."

"Oh yeah." she said taking the keys to her soon to be old car off the ring.

They made conversation while he typed in her info to see about financing. He was attracted to her in a way he hasn't been attracted to a woman since his son's mother when they met. He blinked out of the trance she had him in when the computer notified him of a decision.

"Ok Mrs. Dewitt……"

"Orchid is fine."

"Ok Orchid. With your trade in and excellent credit, we can send you outta here with no down payment. There's just some paperwork we have to do and it's all yours…of course after we get insurance taken care of."

"Great!" she beamed. "Actually, I wanna pay for half of the cost of the car now."

"Hey….what do we have here?" the uninterested co-worker asked walking up after hearing the credit decision.

"Hopefully getting Orchid set up in her new wheels. Am I continuing on?"

"Shit yeah." she said excitedly. "Sorry."

"It's aiight.

"I can take it from here now Javan." he said stepping back expecting Javan to move.

"If you don't mind…I'd like to stick to the sales man I have." Orchid said peeping game.

"Oh okay. So what did you decide on?" he asked trying to be nosey and mask how pissed he was.

"She got the silver Aviator limited edition fully loaded." Javan said with a smirk knowing he was pissed about losing the commission.

"Wow….great car. Well, enjoy your new car. I'm sure Javan will take good care of you. Good day."

"Un huh." she mumbled. "Oh, he needs his ass whipped. I bet he thought I was some hood booger with bad credit and no money. Am I right?"

"That about sums it up. It's cool…I wanted to meet you anyway."

"That's sweet. Looks like I'm leaving out of here with a new car and a new friend."

"I'd prefer the word date." he said looking at her sexily.

"Maybe. We can talk about it after I get my car."

"I know that's right."

Less than an hour later Javan was outside helping Orchid get her belongings from her old car and exchanging phone numbers. She liked Javan, but she was anxious to get in her new car and bump Ledisi.

"Thank you Javan, I love this car already."

"It looks good on you. I'll talk to you soon."
"Yes you will." she said shaking his hand and getting in the car.
She put in her cd, cranked up the music and winked at him before putting on her shades and peeling off. She was in the zone driving down the highway, she felt like she was flying. Wanting an excuse to ride around she headed towards the mall while dialing Kiko.
"What it do bitch!" she yelled into the blue tooth.
"Chillin'......bored as hell. Wsup with you?"
"Chillin' just left mom and D at the airport. Now I'm heading to the mall and then home to dance around in my drawers."
"Unh uh....come get my ass. Keona is with her grandmother and Keon is out with your new peoples. I'm sitting here with my thumb up my ass looking good for no reason." Kiko laughed.
"I'm not too far away from you; I'll be there in less than ten."
        Orchid made an illegal U-turn and took the exit to go back to pick up Kiko. She called to let her know she was pulling up and Kiko was already sitting on the porch. She looked over her glasses until she realized it was Orchid.
"Who's car you done stole?!" she said sashaying to the car.
"Nobody's bitch.....this is mine."
"What! You trade in the XL?"
"Yeah, I was coming from the airport and my check engine light came on. I saw this sexy piece of machinery and took it as a sign. And the salesman was fine as hell...I had the nerve to give him my number."
"Go head girl! Uh oh....Khalil got some

competition!"

"I don't really see it as competition....it's just having options. Besides, I've only been on one date with Khalil."

"Okay player.....options. Listen at you." Kiko said and laughed. "Oh, option number one asked me to bring you to the club tonight. It's his birthday. Please go....you know I don't wanna be around just Keon's sister and them like that." she said turning up her nose.

"I thought ya'll were cool."

"We are, she just pisses me off with some of her comments at times. Anytime she comes to Keon for money and he tells her no, it's my fault. It's always, 'oh, I guess you gotta save money for others in your life.' Dumb bullshit like that and then we supposed to be cool right afterward."

"You say something to Keon?"

"Nah....I got something for that ass though."

After spending a couple hours shopping, they stopped for an early dinner and intruded on the salon, managing to get right in. Orchid dropped Kiko off who made her promise to be at the house by ten to pick her up and drove home.

Chapter 16

Before she got into chill mode, she called to make sure her mom and baby landed safe. After chatting with her mom and a million I love you's from D, she was able to relax. She was lying on the bed smoking an L when her phone rang and she saw it was her Aunt Debbie's house.

"Hey Aunt Deb." she sang into the phone.

"Nah, she in the kitchen. It's Shelle."

"Oh....what's up?"

"I just wanted to call so we can squash all the petty bullshit from the past. I mean...I was a lil outta line last time I saw you but we're family and life is too short."

"I agree but for real Shelle....that was some grimy shit. You should know how much trouble that nigga is from when I was dealing with him."

"I know....I guess I was a lil jealous and the money was good. But I'm sorry and I hope you can one day accept my apology. That's all I wanted to say."

"Shelle.......I accept your apology but actions speak louder than words. This is a start....we just have to see what happens from here."

"I can deal with that. Can I at least come to Lil D's party?"

"Yeah...it's at four. Your mom has an invitation with the location."

"Aiight. I'll see you then." she said and ended the call.

"Aint that something." she said aloud.

After trying on three of the outfits she'd purchased at the mall, Orchid decided on a symmetrical halter stress and wedge sandals that tied up the leg. It was already five after ten, so she threw on her Tiffany and diamond accessories and ran to the car. She'd just started the engine and Kiko called her.

"I'm in the car coming for you now. Five minutes." she yelled into the phone.

"Better be….with your late ass."

Kiko strutted to the car rocking a black and silver Versace number she picked up, looking like she'd just stepped off the runway. She admired her friends' beauty as she approached.

"Alright Ms. Thang." Orchid teased.

"Thank you….thank you. You know my husband likes for me to look good."

"I know how that is."

"Orchid….I'm…."

"Kiko…it's okay. Everyone acts like I'm gonna have a nervous breakdown hearing the word husband or D's name. I'm okay…I've made peace with him being gone. I will always remember him no matter how long he's been gone, but he is the one that's gone and I have to keep living."

"You're right, I'm sorry."

"Don't apologize….you're being my friend and sister. So….can we fire up this blunt and enjoy the night. Shoot, as horny as I been lately, if Khalil plays his cards right he may get some of this."

"Gimme some!"

For someone who was pretty new to the area, there were a lot of people in attendance showing love. Kiko and Orchid walked through the club showing love to those they knew and getting stares from those they didn't. Kiko walked ahead to VIP while Orchid stopped to talk to one of D's boys she hadn't seen since the funeral.

Kiko stepped into VIP and Keon's dick got hard at the sight of her. He knew he'd lucked up when he met her and he had Orchid and D to thank for it. Not liking all the niggas drooling over her as she walked by, he got up to meet her halfway. When he got to her, he took her in his arms and tongued her down....squeezing on her ass.

"Mmmm.....what was that for?" she asked seductively.

"I miss you, I love you......and to let these niggas know, don't even think about it."

"You so hostile.....I love it." she said kissing him again.

"Yo, where Orchid? She ain't wanna come out?"

"She's here. She stopped off to talk to Donovan right quick."

"Oh aiight. Let me get my baby something to drink. Go head to the table, I'll be right there."

Kiko arrived at the table and the whole crew was there. She showed love to all of them before taking a seat in the booth next to Khalil.

"Happy Birthday nigga!" Kiko yelled hugging him.

"Thank you. If you really wanted my birthday to be happy you would've brought me a gift." he said winking, insinuating Orchid.

"Who says I didn't bring that gift with me?"

"Where she at?" he asked looking around.

"Damn. Don't tell me you don't gotten bit by the Orchid bug already." Kiko laughed. "She does have a certain something about her."

"Word up. Is she really here though?"

"Have a look?" she said noticing her walking towards their booth fighting off the hounds. "Damn! Nigga's couldn't wait for her ass to be on the market again." Kiko said aloud unintentionally.

"It's like that?"

"I'm only telling you this cause you like fam, but don't say shit to her. Before she married D, she hadn't fucked with but one nigga. Her mom had her dealing with these preppy niggas that turned out to be bigger assholes than some in the hood. Anyway, when she did start coming around the way and expanding her horizons, D snatched her up before anyone else ever had a chance. She's a good woman."

"I see that."

"She's been through a lot and she still managed to come out on top a better, stronger woman. I wanna be like her when I grow up."

"That's wsup. Sounds like you have mad love for her."

"Mad love is an understatement. She's the yen to my yang and vice versa."

"How long you known her?"

"Since kindergarten….and she's been a bad bitch since then." she said laughing.

"Damn…..can't take fine women nowhere. Niggas don't know how to act but I'll show these mafucka's fucking with my sis. Ain't that right O?"

"That's right. Hey! Happy Birthday Khalil!" Orchid said kissing his cheek and handing him a small box."

"Thanks ma. You ain't have to get me anything."

"I wanted to. Every man needs a pair of those."

"Open that shit up. I wanna see if I got whatever it is." Keon said filling their glasses.

"Aiight….aiight." he said tearing the wrapping paper. "What the fuck?!" he fell out laughing.

"Yooooo….she wild as hell."

"What the fuck is it?" Keon asked trying to see the

box.

"A Pinocchio thong. This shit even has the nose to put your joint in." Khalil said still laughing.

"You know you just wrong for that shit there." Keon said laughing. "Gotta love ya! Come on…drink up. Cheers to my man's birthday and to real family!"

They all tossed back shots and Keon started filling their glasses again.

"I gotta pace myself if I wanna get home in one piece." Orchid warned Keon.

"You ain't gotta go nowhere. My nephew and my princess are chilling and you ain't got shit to do tomorrow. I got you a suite across the street with us. If your ass can't make it across the street, I'm calling AA on that ass."

"You knew about all this bitch?" she pushed Kiko.

"He said it was a possibility but no. And so what if I did." she laughed seeing the shimmer of hope in Khalil's eyes. He'd been wanting to spend some quality time with her but didn't wanna press.

"So….you wanna dance with the birthday boy?"

"Let's get it!"

By one o'clock Kiko and Orchid were feeling it. Keon and Khalil were having a ball just watching them cut up. Khalil spit his drink out when he saw Orchid pulling the rope on the dance floor.

"Yo! She wrong for that one! She wild!" Khalil said laughing looking down at her again.

"You feelin her….ain't you?"

"I mean…."

"Dawg….it's cool. She's a damn good woman. I know you thorough and you like fam…but like I said before. If you just looking for some pussy or you gonna fuck her over….leave her alone. If you really diggin her, then go for it. She need a man and just any nigga ain't gonna do when she's fucked with one of the best."

"I got you dawg. I am feeling her though. I tell you like I tell her and you know me….if I just wanted pussy I can get that. I'm tryna have what you and Kiko got."

"She the one that hooked us up."

"That's wsup."

"Yeah….I'm always gonna owe her for that. I love her ass to death too. Enough about my sis, she speaks for herself……let us get another bottle before they get back. The way they doing it tonight…they may try to drink us dry."

After the club they all stumbled across the highway to the Marriot. Keon gave Orchid the key to her suite which was two doors down from theirs and told her she could have her car keys in the morning. After she slapped him in the back of the head she and Kiko headed into her room.

"I'll be down in a minute babe." Kiko called to Keon, following Orchid into her room. "Here." she said tossing Orchid a box of magnums.

"What are you doing with condoms?!"

"They ain't for me….they're for your ass."

"I don't have a dick to put them on."

"I know…..but Khalil does. Those are just in case you decided to get the "dust knocked off that pussy!" she said mocking Chris Tucker.

"Shut up! You ain't gotta be all loud about it." Orchid laughed. "Anyway, smoke this L with me before you roll out."

"You ain't gotta ask me twice."

They were sitting on the couch in the living room

smoking and talking shit about the hood boogers at the club when Orchid's phone rang. She showed Kiko the phone before she answered it.

"Uh oh!" Kiko souped her up.

"Shut up." she said and slapped her. "Hey."

"What up beautiful? You sleep?"

"Nah, smoking an L with Kiko."

"Oh aiight. I wanted to kick it with you….burn one. I'll catch you later."

"It's cool, she was getting ready to go. Actually Keon's calling the room now. You can come through."

"I'll be there in a minute."

"Aiight, I'm coming…..bye." Kiko ended the call and grabbed her shoes. "King ding a ling is calling. Had the nerve to tell me I was blocking. How am I blocking and Khalil was with his ass."

"He's off the hook. Tell him I'm gonna get him for that in the morning…..make that afternoon." she said and laughed. "Who is it?" she yelled at the door.

"Give me my wife!" Keon yelled.

"You gonna mess around and have these white folks put us out. Stop that." Orchid laughed.

"Smell good up in here. Let me know you got the goodness and ain't sharing." Keon said lighting the rest of the blunt. "Damn girl…..give me some."

"All in my stash." Orchid laughed and dug in her stash to break him off. "Here."

"And you got a sack. I'm coming over tomorrow and smoking all your shit."

"The hell you is!"

"Look like the party's over here." Khalil said peeking in the door, disappointed there was a room full of people.

"Nah….I'm just fucking with my sis about holding out on the good shit. Hit this."

"Okay….this….is aiight." Khalil said inhaling.

"I'm faded and feeling X-rated ma. It's time for us to go."

"Ewwww TMI." Orchid said turning up her nose. "Whatever. I'm riding with you in the morning so don't leave without me."

"I got you."

"Maybe I can drive…..I mean since I'm your bestie and all."

"Her hooptie! Your car better than that toy truck." Keon teased.

"Kiss my ass…..my car was not a hooptie." Orchid laughed.

"Oh no, Ms. Thang got a brand new truck. Rims, TV's…..the whole nine."

"What! I gotta check it out tomorrow. But for now….I gots to roll. Let's bounce ma. See ya'll niggas in a few." Keon walked out with Kiko over his shoulder and her shoes in his hand.

"Bye." she yelled before being carried out the door.

"Those two are off the hook." Khalil said. "They keep my ass laughing."

"Yeah….they're good together. Keon can be an over protective pain in the ass over me at times, but I know he means well. That's my big bruh."

"Yours and mine both. I hope that doesn't mean I'm your brother."

"No….not at all. So, what you been up to?" She asked kicking off her shoes and sitting next to him on the couch.

"Just chillin….getting settled into my new crib."

"Oh, you got a house. Congratulations."

"Thank you. Keon hooked me up with the right

people and it happened. Maybe you can see it some time."

"I'd like that. Your girlfriend wouldn't mind?" she said laughing. He prior told her he didn't have anyone.

"Come on now. You can come over anytime you want. Matter of fact, I'll give you a key."

"That's not necessary, but if you're inviting me over.....I accept."

"I am. Can I ask you a question?"

"Okay."

"What are you looking for? I mean, are you looking to eventually be with someone new?"

"I am. I took the time I needed to mourn D and get my mind right. I knew my life needed to go on and I don't wanna do that alone. So, I took time to get me and my son right and here I am.....ready to move on."

"That's wsup. D was a good dude, I'm sorry he's gone."

"Me too....but I enjoyed the time I had with him and he left me a piece of him in our son. So....I'm good with that."

"You're a strong, beautiful woman....that I wanna get to know better."

"Thank you.....you're pretty beautiful too." she said and laughed. "So what are you into besides the streets?"

"Wow...straight to the point. I like that. I own a couple barbershops.....I'm a beast when it comes to business. Went to school and the whole nine, but needed some start up cash. Then the money got too good and here I am."

"Ever think about getting out the game?"

"Yeah....it's all in the timing. When the opportunity

presents itself for me to get out….I will. Until then, I gotta do what I gotta."

"And no woman huh?"

"I ain't gonna lie and say I aint smash nothing since I been here. That's all it was. These chicks around here, most of them, are on the same shit the chicks were on up top. I can spot them a mile away. So, I been with this join a couple of times and that's it….nothing serious."

"I guess I can give you the benefit of the doubt. I don't wanna be sitting in a room with someone else's man." she laughed.

"If you play your cards right…..I could be your man."

"If I play my cards right?!" she laughed loudly.

"Don't you worry about my cards, they on the table. You just worry about yours."

"Mine are on the table too, shit." he laughed. "You mad cool….I'm digging you." he said taking her hand in his and kissing it.

"I guess you aiight."

"Just aiight." he said smelling her hair, letting his lips graze her neck.

"Maybe….a lil….more than aiight." she said border line moaning. "Can you give me a shot gun?" she said handing him the blunt.

"If you can handle it…yeah."

"Come on with it."

He blew the thick smoke into her mouth as she inhaled. He removed the blunt from his lips and kissed her, not being able to resist being so close to them. She held it as long as she could but ended up coughing and spitting in his face unable to hold the smoke any longer.

"Damn…..you sprayed me." Khalil said laughing.

"I'm so sorry." she said getting up and grabbing him a towel.

"It's cool, that was my fault. I forgot you were holding in smoke. I bet you high as hell right now."

"I got a lil head rush, but I'm good." she said sitting down on the chaise lounge near the window.

"Why you sit way over there?"

"I wanted to stretch my legs and didn't want to have my feet all over you."

"You can put whatever you want on me….except shit." he laughed.

"Come over here then." she said sexily.

"I don't know what'll happen with me being so close to you."

"Whatever I allow to happen."

He walked over to the chaise lounge next to Orchid before leaning over to kiss her. She wrapped her arms around his neck and allowed his tongue to dance with hers, causing a moan to escape her throat. He ran his fingers through her long soft hair before lightly tugging it and planting kisses on her neck.

"Orchid…..can I taste you?" he asked between kisses.

"If you taste me…..I may want more than that."

"Only if you want it ma." he said reaching under her dress and pulling off her already wet panties when she didn't object. He raised her short dress not wanting to get ahead of himself by taking it off. He kissed and sucked on the inside of her thighs before flicking his tongue across her clit and tasting her juices for the first time. He lifted her, grabbing her ass with both hands and began licking figure eights around her clit. She moaned his name, arching her back as he brought her to multiple orgasms and still kept going. She was damn near yelling when he began playing with her spot and sucking on her clit. Her legs began shaking and the rest of her body followed suit as she approached her biggest climax. "Khalil......yes! Yes!" she yelled as her juices ran from her.

"Sweeter than chocolate." he said licking his lips. His dick was so hard it hurt, but he wanted her to let him know she was ready. Orchid stood on unsteady legs and peeled the rest of her clothes off standing in front of him. He stood and slowly began taking off his clothes. When they both stood there naked he kissed her and she enjoyed tasting her juices on his lips.

"You....got...a condom?" she asked.

"Shit....I gotta go get some." he said pissed. "I wasn't expecting this to happen."

"Lucky for you someone else was." she said finding the box of magnums amongst the scattered clothing.

"Remind me to thank who ever that was." he said kissing her and backing towards the bedroom. He turned her around and laid her on the middle of the bed on her back. He wanted to taste her again....her pussy was definitely addictive.

"Khalil....I can't......"

"Yes you can......come for me again." he said spreading her legs and sucking again on her clit. He ate her pussy so good; she shed tears of joy when she had her orgasm. She licked her lips in anticipation as he stroked his bulging dick while she opened the condom. He lowered himself on to her and kissed her again...looking into her eyes. "I'm not looking for a one night stand ma."

"I'm not either but....we'll just have to see what happens from here."

"I can deal with that." he said and entered her tight walls. He closed his eyes and could've sworn he'd died and gone to heaven. He imagined what she would feel like from the moment he laid eyes on her, but he underestimated.

"Shit….Orchid." he moaned as she raised her ass, working her pussy. "Fuck….Do that shit ma." Orchid was in the zone…enjoying the feeling of him inside of her, filling her up. Feeling it, Orchid turned over and began riding him slowly while he sucked on her taut nipples. "Oh this pussy is good…..shit!" he moaned as her movements sent currents throughout his whole body. He thrust towards her hitting her walls until she began moaning loudly and he felt her pussy tightening on his dick. "Come for me ma…" he said playing with her clit while she did her thing. She felt him swelling inside her and knew he was coming. She picked up the pace feeling herself about to come. He exploded buckets into the condom, not wanting to leave her body.

She laid on his chest with his arms around her, sweating and trying to catch her breath. She had completely blown his mind and he couldn't feel his legs he nutted so hard.

"That shit was intense." he said breathing heavy.

"You okay?" he asked running his fingers through her damp hair.

"Yeah." she said winded. "I tell you one thing, toys ain't got nothing on some real, good dick." she said and laughed.

"You wild." he laughed with her. "I love the way you feel. Like your body was made custom for me."

"I guess we did do the damn thing pretty good huh?"

"Did we."

"I'm gonna shower, I done worked up a sweat." she said and kissed him.

He watched the sweat glisten on her naked body as she walked to the bathroom and he became aroused again. He ordered some room service for them, grabbed another condom, and had it on by the time he got to the shower.

"I got something else I wanna give you." he said stepping in and kissing her.

He grabbed her ass, lifting her against the wall and entered her again. He thrust into her hungrily, causing them to both moan out of control. It's only been one night and he was hooked already. Having his second wind, he carried her out of the shower back to the bed still dripping wet. He laid her on her back, placing her legs over his shoulders and stroked her while playing with her clit.

"Shit….Kha…lil…oh God!" she moaned as he stroked her silly.

"Fuck…..ma. Work that….shit." he moaned as she began working her pussy again. His legs became weak as she tightened her walls around him and came. Her wetness sent him over the edge, cumming and shaking as he kissed her. They laid on the bed wrapped in each other's arms talking until room service came. She sat on the bed wrapped in a towel as he fed her fruit and they talked. By the time they'd closed their eyes, they were feeling each other a lot more.

Chapter 17

Neither getting too much sleep, Kiko and Orchid approached the elevator wearing dark glasses and their hair in ponytails. They boarded the elevator with not so much as a word to each other until they reached the downstairs coffee shop to get their fix.

"So….how'd your visit with Khalil go after we left?" Kiko asked blowing her coffee.

"It was nice. We got to know each other a lil better." she said blowing her coffee avoiding Kiko's stare. She knew her better than she knew herself, so she knew she was checking her out behind her dark frames.

"You fucked him…didn't you?!" she said excitedly.

"You already know what the answer is so why ask?"

"Okay!" she said slapping her five. "So….was it good?"

"It was better than good. I don't know if it's because it's been over five years since I had dick or what but when I tell you I had multiples every time……whooo!"

"Every time? How many times ya'll fuck?"

"Three or four I think."

"Okayyy! Orchid got her groove back. So, how do you feel?"

"I'm good. You know I was scared I might have a flashback and call out D's name….but I was good. We cuddled and talked after, fed each other…..it was cool."

"So I guess you gonna fuck him again than huh?"

"I think I can see that in the near future."

"Gimme some!"

The next couple of weeks were bananas for Orchid. She had to finish up arrangements for D's party and put the finishing touches on Keon and Kiko's wedding which was a week later. Since D's party didn't start until four and it wasn't at her home, she was able to sleep in a lil….or so she though.

"Mom! Wake up!" Lil D shook her. "Go me….it's my birthday! Go me…"

"Boy…what you in here doing?" she laughed picking him up and tickling him on the bed.

"Grandma said for you to get your butt up and come eat. The flower man came for you too."

"The flower man?"

"Yeah. He said your name and Grandma took the flowers from him. They downstairs."

"They're downstairs."

"Yes. You coming?"

"Let me brush my teeth and I'll be right there."

She got downstairs and there was indeed an arrangement of flowers on the table. She grabbed the card and went into the kitchen where she heard voices.

"I should've known your ass would be over here eating my mama's breakfast." Orchid teased Kiko.

"Hey Aunt Orchid." Keona ran over and hugged her leg.

"How's my lil girlfriend doing? You ready to party."

"Yup…we got D a gift too."

"Cool."

"Mommy can we go play?"

"Did ya'll eat already?"

"Yes!" they answered in unison.

"Okay…have fun. " Orchid said and laughed.

"Morning mom."

"Good morning and there goes your coffee."
Theresa laughed. "I might have to get me one of
those trucks you got. That is so me."

"Like mother like daughter." Kiko laughed.

"Shut up. Where's your other half?"

"He's gonna meet us there. Him and your boo."

"What? You gotta boo?" Theresa shrieked.

"He's not my boo. He's someone I been getting to
know."

"Is that who sent the flowers?" Theresa asked being
nosey.

"Yes, if you must know."

"Can't wait to meet him. There's the pancakes,
eggs and sausage....if ya'll want anything else you
better fix it. I'm gonna go get dressed. Orchid, I
suggest you do the same sometime soon."

"Yes mother." she said sarcastically.

"Still gotta run shit huh?" Kiko laughed.

"You know that shit ain't gonna change."

"So, wsup with you and Khalil? I thought you were
feeling him."

"I am....I just haven't had the time to really kick it
with him lately. And I don't want him to meet D
until and if we decided to get a lil closer. I won't
have my son calling niggas uncle." Orchid laughed.

"I feel that. Well he misses you. I think he's pussy
whipped personally." Kiko laughed. "Maybe both."

"Girl, I've been thinking about that dick! The sex
was off the chain."

"Get you some more then."

"I might see if my mom will keep D while we go
out. Lord knows I'm gonna need a drink after
dealing with a room from of kids."

"I'll drink to that."

Orchid got a lil emotional watching D and his family interact. They'd missed out on five years of birthday parties and family gatherings. She felt like she had taken those things from him but she also did what she had to do to be a better, stronger person and mom. She stood with teary eyes and a smile on your face.

"I know what you're thinking and don't make yourself feel bad. You did what you needed to do. If I can forgive you for leaving me for five long, long years....all is forgiven. Besides, you are both here with me now." Kiko said putting her arm around Orchid and hugging her.

"See....that's why I love you."

"Say cheese!" Theresa said taking their pictures. "Do you two ever get tired of each other?" she asked laughing.

"Nope" they said in unison.

"I envy your relationship. This friendship goes beyond just that. You two are one in the same, blood.....my two pains in the asses." she laughed.

"Aww.....love you ma." Kiko said kissing her.

"Me too." added Orchid.

"You better. Ya'll been running around this party after these kids like crazy. I'll keep them tonight and ya'll can go see strippers or whatever it is ya'll crazy asses do. Just don't get pregnant for pete's sake." Theresa laughed. "Look at that boy! D......what in the sam hills....." she said stomping off without another word.

"She is a mess. Looks like you didn't have to ask and I don't need to find a sitter either. We might as well double."

"You work out the details with your husband. Khalil might not speak to me after I hit it and ran."

Orchid said and burst out laughing.

"You sure did! Hot ass mess!"

Having the party away from the house was definitely a good look. After everything was said and done, parents took their kids and all they needed to do was carry out gifts and bounce. One gift D was not letting going off was the custom made diamond and platinum chain. Orchid reamed him out about that but Keon insisted his lil man's had a bomb piece for his neck.

After a few dirty looks and a kiss Khalil was back on team Orchid. They were all over each other in the parking lot after he let her have it about sexually abusing him. She had to laugh thinking back at the conversation she and Kiko had earlier. She promised to meet him at the spot they agreed on before they parted ways.

Orchid was browsing through her closet trying to decide on something to wear while D played in the Jacuzzi. Leave it to Kiko to change up plans, she had an hour less to get her life together and be ready by the time she arrived with Keona. She was pulling the skirt and blouse out of the closet she was wearing when her mom walked in with a glass of wine for them both.

"So…..all I wanna know is, who was that fine ass man you were talking to at the party? If I was younger, or a cougar, I'd have to holla at him."

"Damn that BET!' Orchid laughed.

"What?"

"Ma….."

"Girl please, I was a woman before I was your mother. And….it's been five years since D passed. I think it's time you get a man. I saw them toys you got." Theresa fell out laughing.

"Mom!" Orchid shrieked. "I can't believe you!" she doubled over laughing.

"I'm serious. Shit, I got me a lil friend back home. A sister has needs."

"I know that's right." Orchid said giving her a high five. "For your information…..I'm going out with him tonight. He's Keon's step brother."

"Keon's mom is married?! That lady is a mess."

"That is not nice…..and no, not anymore. He's her ex's son, but they were always close. Anyway, we've been chillin'….if you wanna call it that."

"Soooo…..you like him? I bet he has a nice body."

"That is enough outta you and yeah….I like him a lil something." she answered and smiled.

"Good, I hoped you'd start dating again. Way to grab the bull by the horns. You still should've got some." Theresa said and laughed.

"Actually…..I did." Orchid said with a smirk.

"Heyyyy!" her mom high fived her. "Don't give me details but was he good?"

"I can't believe you……yeah, he was."

"Just good or damn good?"

"Let's just say, it was one of those rare occurrences where tears spill from your eyes."

"I knew it!" Theresa yelled.

"Just nasty!" Orchid laughed.

"Mom! I'm ready to get out!" D yelled.

"Here I come!" she yelled back. "If you have no other questions about my sex life, I'm gonna get your grandson out the tub."

"That's it for now. I got him after you get him out so you can get ready for that man…..and wear something sexier than that. I've seen school teachers wearing outfits like that."

"Ma….that's Dior." Orchid said with her hand on her hips.

"Well tell Mr. Dior to stop making outfits for teachers." Theresa cracked up. "I'm just messing baby. Why don't you wear that sexy little dress you picked up at the mall yesterday? I might have to get me some spanx and borrow that."

"Oh hell no! I might have to move out to Arizona to keep a closer eye on you."

"The hell you are. You stay your ass right here in Jersey and get that man. I got this." she said walking away. "I'll be back up to get D." she yelled going down the stairs.

"Ain't that a bitch." she mumbled walking into the bathroom. "Is my birthday boy all clean?"

"Yup. I had fun mom! When can I have another party?"

"Next year on your birthday. But the summer is coming and we'll have plenty of parties in the back yard."

"Yeah. Do I get more gifts?"

"Not that type of party and you haven't even opened the ones you got today and you already asking for more."

"Can I open them?"

"Yes. Grandma will help you. I'm going out with Aunt Kiko for a little while."

"Yeah…..me and grandma say you need more fun."

"What!?" she laughed. "I have plenty of fun with you here at home."

"I have fun too….but sometimes I just wanna watch cartoons."

"Listen at you. Come on so we can put your night clothes on."

"I love you."

"I love you too D."

Orchid took her moms' advice and put on the black lace halter dress she'd picked up. She had to admit....it was a good choice. She pulled her shoulder length hair up into a twist, leaving a few curls hanging and was impressed. She heard the door bell and headed downstairs knowing Kiko'd be rushing her.

"Well lookey here, someone is ready......and looking fierce!"

"Thank you, thank you. You're looking very Fashion week yourself."

"See....I told you to wear that. Look at your ass." Theresa said slapping it.

"Stop beating my donkey." Orchid said and they laughed. "Don't be watching none of that filth you watch with my baby ma. Oh and he wants to open gifts."

"I got this. You worry about getting that man so you can throw away those B.O.B's you got in that room." Theresa laughed.

"Ma T.....what you know about that?" Kiko asked cracking up.

"Oh, I knows. You need money for condoms?" Theresa joked. "I'm just playing. I'm just tickled about you and that man. Exciting."

"Stay out my weed and no more wine." Orchid said laughing.

"Be safe....love you."

"Love you too."

Khalil had to throw back his shot to keep his mouth from dropping open when Orchid and Kiko walked in. Orchid was beautiful but to him, she was even more so than the last time. He chilled in the cut watching her as she moved closer and got pissed when other niggas tried to touch her. To him Orchid was already his…..because he had no plans on letting her go.

"Uh oh….party over here!" Keon yelled hugging Orchid before kissing Kiko. "Uh! We might skip this shit, go back home and go half on another one with your fine ass."

"Slow your roll….I need a drink."

"You know I got you baby. O, what's my lil man doing?"

"Him and Keona should be opening gifts with my crazy ass mother. You know he will not take off that chain. He just took a bath with it on."

"He's not supposed to. I'mma get him a pinky ring soon."

"My baby is not a pimp." Orchid laughed.

"He will be. And what you do to my mans?" Keon laughed.

"Leave her alone Keon." Kiko slapped him.

"Nothing that wasn't done to you a long time ago." Orchid laughed.

"Nah…uh….let's get a drink. I can't even say shit." he laughed leading the way.

They approached the booth and Khalil stood up so Orchid could get in. He smelled her before she was close to him and the smell intoxicated him more.

"Didn't think I was gonna come….did you?" she said before pecking his lips softly.

"If you didn't I was gonna come looking for you." he laughed. "You look good enough to eat." he said leaning into her.

"Mmmm….do tell."

"You coming home with me tonight?"

"I'll have to think about it."

"You know you driving me crazy right now. Look what you do to me." he said guiding her hand under the table to feel his bulging dick.

"Feels…..nice."

"Could feel even better. So…..what ya'll ladies drinking?"

"It's about time you acknowledged my presence….damn."

"My bad Kiko….you know I love you." he said kissing her cheek.

"Hey….get your own nigga." Keon pulled Kiko to him and laughed. "Ay Lil….let's go holla at this cat right quick."

"You not gonna run off are you?" Khalil asked.

"I'll be around."

"Look at ya'll. If ya'll could've fucked in this booth, you probably would've." Kiko laughed. "The sex was like that?!"

"It was like that."

"Hey, I'll drink to that shit!" Kiko touched her glass with Orchids'.

After a few more glasses and a lot more shit talking, they hit the floor. Orchid wasn't too beat to dance with any of the fellas that approached, Kiko was her partner. Orchid was all into the music, so didn't realize she had a partner behind her. She turned around when she bumped into a pelvis and saw it was Javan, her car salesman.

"Orchid….how you doin' ma?" he asked hugging her.

"I'm good and yourself? You look different."

"I do me when I'm off the clock….but I'm good. You look good girl, damn."

"Thank you. You know I'm in love right?"

"Is that right?"

"My car is the bomb.com. If I could sleep with it at night I would." she laughed.

"Car can't keep you warm. Actually, yeah it can." he laughed. "So when you gonna let me take you out? I never got that phone call."

"I've been crazy busy lately. I'll give you a call tomorrow maybe."

"Ahem!" Kiko cleared her throat.

"My bad. Kiko, this is Javan…..Javan, this is my other half, my best friend Kiko."

"Nice to meet you. Can I get ya'll a drink?"

"We have something upstairs, thanks." Orchid politely declined.

"Actually, I'm gonna go get me a drink."

"I'm right behind you."

"Aiight. Nice meeting you Javan."

"Nice meeting you too. Well, since I didn't get that phone call can I at least get a dance?"

"I can do that."

Khalil was not happy that she was talking to a nigga as long as she was or that they were now dancing. He had to be easy though. She was not his girl, so he couldn't trip. Not caring to see anymore, he went back to the booth and rolled an L. By the time he set fire to it, Orchid was sliding next to him in the booth.

"Damn, what you do run up here?" he asked.

"No, I glided gracefully. The song ended and I needed a refill."

"Who was that guy?" Kiko asked loudly.

"That's the guy that sold me my lovely new automobile." she said dancing in her seat. "Can I get another shot gun?" she asked a now calm Khalil.

"The last time I gave you one, I ended up with my face between those beautiful thighs." he said kissing her neck.

"Ask me again?"

"Ask wh….. You coming home with me?"

"Unh huh." she moaned and kissed him after her shot gun.

"We might have to cut this night short."

After some of the evening girl talk, Orchid hugged her big brother and Kiko before getting into Khalil's Benz coup. Orchid toyed with the stereo until she found something she liked and sat back in her seat. They laughed and talked the half hour it took to get to his house. Yeah……she was feeling him but was determined to take things slow.

"Wow, this is nice Khalil." she said walking into the house.

"Thanks, it's not done yet though."

"It's nice…not too much. I was expecting a flat screen, leather sofa, PS3 and a king sized bed.' she giggled.

"Awww….it's like that? You wild." Khalil laughed. "You want a drink?"

"I guess I can drink a lil yak. I know it's kinda late but do you have any serial killer, rapist, sexual deviant, mental instability or Ike Turner issues?"

"Did you say all that shit in one breath?" he laughed.

"Don't worry about it….answer the question."

"To be perfectly honest…..no. None of the above. Anything else you wanna know?"

"Are you gonna make me come the way you did that night?" she said closing the space between them and kissing his lips.

"Nah…..I plan on improving on that experience. You know you sexy as hell?"

"Thank you. So……" she said massaging his dick

through his khaki's. "…..where's my drink?"

"Damn…..you fucking me up right now. I'mma get that for you…get comfortable."

"Where's the bathroom?"

"The door right there." he pointed and adjusted his dick. "Shit!"

"Huh?" she yelled.

"Nah, nothing. If you wanna go upstairs, there's a living room up there. At the end of the hall."

He took a phone call from Keon before he joined Orchid upstairs. She was on the couch with her shoes off, flipping through channels.

"I didn't know if you wanted a chaser or not but I brought one anyway."

"Thank you. I know you have some movies up in here. Or do you just wanna fuck and then drop me off?" she said trying not to laugh but it didn't work.

"Damn."

"What?! If I had my way, a woman like you would be here in my bed every night waiting on me to come in and make that pussy talk." he said winking at her. "I treat women the way they deserve to be treated….like queens. If I was on some straight fucking shit, you might get that but you……I'm trying to make part of my world."

"I uh….I do like you Khalil. I just need to take more time before I can commit to being with you."

"I'm not saying right now. We can take it at whatever pace you want. Beggers can't be choosers." he said and smiled.

"Good answer." she said kissing him.

They sat on the couch in each others' arms just talking, getting to know one another. Orchid was even able to talk about D with him and be comfortable with it. After talking to her, Khalil was feeling her on a whole other level. Not only was attracted to her but he admired her, respected her. She was definitely a keeper, so he opened up about his dealings with his baby mother. By the end of their conversation, all cards were laid on the table and neither of them was running for cover.

"Do you mind if I take a shower? I also need something to sleep in."

"I got you. I was gonna do the same, it was hot in that bitch tonight. Use my bathroom, I'll leave something on the bed for you."

"I hope you not bringing me some old girlfriends' nightie."

"Come on now. It's one of my t-shirts. We need to get you on comic view."

When Khalil walked in his bedroom Orchid was in his t-shirt laying in the middle of the bed laughing at the television. He licked his lips as he watched her breasts move under the cotton. He tossed his towel on the couch, put on some boxers, and laid next to her.

"You smell good." he said kissing her shoulder.

"Yeah, Degree body wash for men doesn't smell too bad."

"I'll have some Caress or Victoria's secret over here for you next time you come."

"Oh, I get an advance invite. Uh oh."

"You accepting?"

"Yeah…..I accept." she said laying on her back and looking into his brown eyes.

"What?"

"I just wanted to look at you. Do you know how sexy you are?" she said pushing him back and straddled him.

"No….you gonna tell me."

"I'm gonna show you."

Orchid kissed his lips slow and sexy until their lips had to separate so he could pull the oversized t-shirt over her hair. He turned her over and kissed her more deeply, offering her his tongue to play with. Starting at her neck, he placed soft kisses and simple bites along her body until he got to her thighs. He kissed and sucked on the gateway to his heaven until they opened on their own. He smiled mischievously and licked his lips before he began flicking his tongue across her clit and she began to moan. He enjoyed teasing her as he would suck on her clit and pull back. "Stop....tea..sing me." she moaned as he fingered her spot.

"I got you playa." he said and sucked the lips around her clit causing her to gasp in pleasure. "Shit.....eat....this....pussy! Damn Khalil!" she moaned. Her moans only turned him on more, causing him to ravage her pussy. She shook, moaned, and begged him to stop but he continued until she was screaming his name..."Khalil!.....Oh...my God! Oh..." and coming all over his face. Even after she orgasmed and laid limp, he licked around her clit some more as he stroked his already hard dick. He slid the condom on and slid between her legs, kissing her as his dick moved across her clit having her damn near speechless.

"How...am I...doing so far?" he asked between kisses.

"Damn good." she moaned.

"You want some of this big dick or can I taste you some more?"

"Gimme the.....dick baby. Damn!" she moaned as she felt her clit swelling.

"I'mma give it to you....after I taste you again." he

said going back to sucking on her clit. She tried to fight the heat that took over her body and the release of her nectar without success. She squeezed her breasts as she had her fourth orgasm and she hadn't gotten the dick yet.

Not giving her a chance to catch her breath, he entered her, stroking her slowly as he kissed her lips and neck.

"Damn….you feel….so good." he moaned. "Damn ma!" he said as she began to throw her wet pussy at him.

She managed to get on top and began riding him slowly and seductively. He sucked on her breasts as she rode his dick like a champion jockey. His toes were twitching and he was moaning her name. "Damn Orchid…..fuck! You….so…wet! Ahhhh shit!" he growled as he felt himself about to erupt. "Fuck! Damn….this shit is….big. Work that shit…..ahhhh…..ahhhhh…..ahhhhhhhh!" he moaned loudly as she milked him dry.

She laid on his chest panting and sweaty with his arms wrapped around her. He was tracing her sweaty back with his finger as he enjoyed the feeling of her soft body against his. She looked into his face and smiled sweetly, too tired to speak.

"You…..are my dream. You know that?"

"I guess I know now." she said and smiled.

"I'm not trying to scare you off by saying that. You just seem to be everything I look for in a woman…..and now that I see my dream can be a reality, a nigga got hope."

"Khalil….that's so sweet." she said and kissed him. "I think you're pretty fly your damn self. We may be able to do a lil something." she said jokingly while teasing him with her nipples dangling just within reach of his lips. She felt him harden between her legs and she immediately became wet. Not able to resist, he took her nipple into his mouth. "Hand me another one of those things." he said referring to a condom. She tore it open with her teeth, slid it on, and inserted him inside of her. "Looks like another long night, huh?" she said. "Looks like it."

Chapter 18

Although they didn't spend as much time as he'd like, Khalil and Orchid were spending more time together. She'd yet to introduce him to Lil D because she wanted to wait and see where their relationship was going.

Glad the day had finally arrived, Orchid packed overnight bags for she and Lil D before heading to the hotel to check in. She'd managed to find a beautiful resort about an hour away and the set up was perfect. She was able to get Kiko and Keona to come along without her getting suspicious or asking questions.

"D....you ready to go?" she yelled.

"Yes mom!" he yelled and walked into her bedroom. "We going in our new car? Can I bring Shrek?"

"Yes you can.....and we'll go down and pack some snacks for the ride."

"Yeah! Mommy, you're the best!" he said hugging her leg and taking off.

They pulled up in front of Keon and Kiko's house and D took off inside before she could put the car in park. Keon was at the door showing all 32's with open arms.

"Hey! Wsup Lil man?"

"Chillin' Uncle K. We going on a trip!"

"Yeah, I heard. Look....." he said pulling out some money. "....here's a couple of dollars for your pocket. Buy your mom and them some lunch on the way there and keep the rest for yourself. You remember what those are?"

"Benjamins!" he said excitedly waving the two hundreds in the air. "Thanks!" he said giving him dap.

"My man. Keona's in her room."

"Okay!" he yelled and took off running.

"I know you ain't over here giving that boy more money."

"Damn skippy! Gotta keep my soldier laced." he said and laughed. "Awww….don't feel bad, I got a lil something for you too…..but you gotta wait to get it."

"It better be worth the wait all this work you done had me doing lately. You lucky I love your ass."

"You better. Your boy on the way over here."

"Tell him hello. We'll be leaving in the next five minutes; I'm not trying to hit a traffic jam. If your wife ain't ready, I'm leaving her ass."

"Like hell you is! I got a bachelor party to attend tonight." he said doing the two step. "Anyway, everything is paid for, all ya'll gotta do is check in and the rest is on me. Everyone else will be arriving tomorrow morning so keep that ass busy."

"I got this! Now move, so I can see my niece."

Paying extra for the televisions and DVD's in the truck was definitely worth it. Keona and D were in the back with their head phones on watching Shrek and we were able to talk shit and listen to music.

"Girl! I needed this little get away. Keon been driving me nuts."

"He loves you and you love him."

"True….but his ass been clingy as hell lately. I think I may have brush burns on my pussy from so much fucking." Kiko said and laughed.

"Lucky you."

"Please, I know Khalil been knocking the bottom outta that ass." Kiko laughed.

"Do he! Well, when we have time."

"I don't know why the hell you busting your ass at that job anyway. To be perfectly honest, you don't need the money. D always made sure you were taken care of and you're smart with money. Bitch, you know you loaded."

"Yeah, but I don't want to just sit around doing nothing all day. Besides, you never know what can happen."

"Bitch, do you or do you not have at least seven figures in your account?"

"But...."

"Answer the question."

"You know the answer to that."

"Okay...so what the hell do you think could possibly happen that would wipe you out? You can volunteer somewhere; start that jewelry line you always wanted to do. Anything you want to do, you can.....and you'll succeed."

"See.....that's why you're my best friend. I'll think about it."

"All I wanna think about is that in room massage I plan on getting when we get there."

"I heard that."

"Mommy...I'm hungry." D said.

"Ok, we'll stop off somewhere to grab something."

"I'm hungry too." Keona chimed in.

"I'll buy you something....I got Benjamins." D said proudly.

"I have...Benjamins."

"Sorry."

"Where he get Benjamins from?" Kiko asked laughing.

"Your damn husband! I done told him about that. He gonna mess around and get my baby jacked."

"You know he likes spoiling him. I think it's cute."
"You would."

After the kids were asleep they were able to get loose. Shaunie drove up to join her as well as Kiko's cousin Jan and they had a little bachelorette party of their own. Not able to get too rowdy with the kids in one of the bedrooms, they settled for drinks, a lil smoke, and in room massages. Orchid made sure to tip their therapists extra so they'd keep the weed smell on the qt.

After they were done with their massages they sat around in their plush robes talking about their favorite topics....men, sex, and more sex. They were discussing toys, positions, and oral sex.....falling over each other in laughter. Orchid's cell rang and she picked it up still laughing.

"You better not be over there feeling on no strippers. That only dick that belongs in those hands....is mine." Khalil said in the phone and laughed.

"Shut up....and there is not any strippers over here. Ladies only....and we don't need strippers to have a good time, thank you."

"Aiight, aiight....all that mouth. I bet you if I was there, the only thing I'd hear coming out of you would be moaning. Smart ass!" he said laughing.

"Whatever......Mr. "What the fuck are you doing to me?" Orchid laughed.

"Ah....okay. You got that......you got that." he laughed. "You miss me?"

"Yeah....I guess I miss you."

"I guess I take that. So....I get to finally meet your mom huh?"

"Yeah....she should be getting here any minute."

"That's wsup. You know you gonna have to sneak

to see me so I can do some things to you when I get there right?"

"Just call me and I'll be there."

"Aiight, I'mma let you enjoy you're evening. I'll be going home with blue balls since my pussy is out of town."

"Your pussy huh?"

"I'm the only one in it….right?"

"Most definitely….you ain't even gotta ask."

"Aiight then….that's my pussy and this is your dick. 'Cause I damn sure ain't giving this dick to anyone else. You got me strung out like a two dollar crack hoe. Shit!" he said laughing. "Aiight ma….I holla."

"Awwww…..must've been Khalil." Shaunie teased.

"Shut up….and yes, it was."

"Khalil…..you fucking with fine ass Khalil." Jan perked.

"Yes and no."

"Yes and no my ass! They both pussy whipped." Kiko said laughing.

"Kiss my ass." Orchid laughed. "Stop talking shit and let's crack open this other bottle. Hold that thought." Kiko said opening the door.

"I heard ya'll big mouth asses all the way at the elevator! Hey baby" Theresa hugged Orchid.

"Hey ma. Come on in and join the party."

"Mom T! What are you doing here?" Kiko jumped up hugging her. "Awww… now this is a party."

"You know it. Shaunie….nice to see you. Long time no see." she said hugging Shaunie.

"Nice to see you too. You look good."

"Thank you….I'm trying to keep up with my daughter. Especially after seeing that fine ass man she had over last time."

"Ohhh! Listen at her." Shaunie said laughing. "Mom T, this is my cousin Jan. Jan this is Orchids' mom Theresa…..my second mother."

"Nice to meet you Ms. Theresa."

"Nice to meet you. So…where's my babies?"

"In there knocked out." Kiko answered adding, "thank the lord."

"Aww….well, I'll spoil them tomorrow. Tonight, I'm getting my drink on!"

Orchid had to take two aspirin that morning and get on her job. She burst into Kiko's bedroom and snatched off the covers, having a tug of war with her.

"Get your ass up, we got things to do. And…I'm going to wake those other bitches up too." Orchid said finally winning almost pulling her off the bed.

"Can a bitch at least have some coffee? Damn!"

"We can have coffee when we get downstairs to breakfast. I got everything set up. Now move your ass." she said walking out of the room.

"Morning mommy!" D perked.

"Morning baby." She picked him up to hug him.

"Mom!" he whined and then laughed.

"What, 'cause you're eight I can't pick you up anymore."

"Yup! I'm a big boy…but I like it sometimes. Can we have breakfast?"

"Yes, we're all going to breakfast and then Grandma is taking you and Keona swimming."

"Who is Aunt Orchid?" Keona said running out of the room.

"Yes…but we gotta get dressed, so let's go."

Orchid invaded everyone's else's room hearing moans and groans from everyone. They hadn't gone to sleep until almost four am and here she was at nine thirty waking them up.

They resembled the Klumps going into the breakfast buffet Orchid had set up. Everyone was starving and in need of caffeine fix. Kiko made a bee line for the coffee station before filling her plate with pork of all kinds and heading back to the table. "So…Miss Drill instructor, why are we up'so early?" Kiko asked sipping on her coffee.

"Because we have shit to do today. I have a surprise for you and all you have to do is follow my lead and ask no questions. If you cause problems the whole thing is off and I'm taking your ass home. Got me?" Orchid said looking serious.

"Well damn….maybe you need my cup of coffee too." Kiko laughed. "Alright….I'll play along, but this better be good."

"Trust me….it is. Alright, let's get our eat on so we can get this show on the road." Orchid perked.

After breakfast they got right to it. Kiko was blindfolded before she was led into the honeymoon suite that she and Keon would be occupying later that evening to get her ready. The makeup artist took her into the smaller bathroom to do her face before the blindfold was put back on and she was led into the dressing room. Orchid left Shaunie in charge and slipped away to tell Keon about himself for arriving late. They had an hour and a half before the ceremony was supposed to start and he and his crew had just arrived at the resort.

"Who!?" he yelled from behind the door.

"You better open this door!"

"Shit!" he said aloud before opening the door.

"Don't start tripping O. We over slept."

"Do you know how long you have to get ready?"

"A couple hours….why?"

"Nooooo…..the ceremony starts in now, an hour and twenty minutes. So, you have no time to smoke this blunt…." she said snatching it from his hand. "….or drinking. Get your ass dressed and be ready by the time I come back." she said walking towards the door.

"Can I at least have my blunt back?"

"Hell no! That's the price you pay for messing with the wedding planner." she said holding back a laugh.

"Damn…I thought we was better than that. A nigga can't get a hug….kiss, nothing? I think I'm a lil offended." Khalil said crossing his arms like a toddler.

"Aww….my bad baby." she said and kissing him slowly. "You better get your ass together too. I ain't playin'" she said and walked out the door.

"Uh! I think I like it when she takes charge." Khalil said grinning.

"Nigga, I don't wanna hear about nothing sexual you doing with my sis."

"I was just sayin'….."

"Don't say shit. Just roll another L, since her ass took that one. Ain't that a bitch!"

They were gonna get started about five minutes behind schedule but Orchid could live with that. She had to pat herself on the back, she did the damn thing. Their colors were Tiffany Blue and White. Getting caught up in some of the wedding shows on television, she got some good ideas. Their cake was stacked Tiffany boxes of different sizes and their keepsakes came inside a miniature version, a small silver framed picture of Keon and Kiko when they'd gotten engaged. Not wanting to overdo it with the blue, the small bridal parties dresses were white, with blue accents. Kiko's dress....a simple but beautiful off white halter. She knew they'd both be happy with what she'd done.

Chapter 19

It was show time! After making sure Keon was where he needed to be and the wedding party in place, Orchid took Kiko downstairs just as the music was about to begin. She put her in place and just smiled at her friend. She envied her at this moment, but wasn't sad. She and D had a beautiful wedding and the time they had together was even more beautiful…..and she vowed to have that again.
"Ok….I'm gonna take off the blind fold now. I owe you a shot or two for behaving." she laughed as she carefully took off the blind fold.
"Thank the…..Lord." she said as her eyes came in focus. "Orchid….what is all this?! Did you….."
"Well not all by myself, your husband opened his wallet and let me dig in a lil something'. The rest is all me…..with some help from Santa's helpers." she said smiling.
"Orchid….I don't know what to say." she said with tears in her eyes.
"Don't say anything….you ain't seen nothing yet. Now stop crying, you have to take pictures." she said dabbing her eyes. "Alright….see you out there. You come in when you hear you're song."
"What song?"
"You'll remember when you hear it." she said taking her place next to Khalil.
"Did I tell you how beautiful you look?" he asked eyeing her seductively.
"No….but thank you." she said and kissed him.
"Alright Keona….D. You're on."
Orchid watched with a smile on her face as her handsome son and beautiful niece made their way down the aisle looking like pros as the music to

Jagged Edge's, "Let's Get Married" featuring Rev Run played. She chuckled as she noticed Keon getting jiggy with it at the altar. After the small party had taken their places, the doors reopened, and Kiko made her way towards her husband to "Trading My Life" by R. Kelly. When Orchid was in her view she pointed at her to let her know she was on point. She'd always talked about wanting to walk down the aisle to that song.

Kiko was pleasantly surprised to see her closest friends and family in attendance. Orchid had covered all bases…and had blown Keon and Kiko away. Keon couldn't wait until the end of the ceremony to kiss his bride, so he took the opportunity to do so before the officiator said a word.

The ceremony, short and sweet with just a pledge of eternal love being sited and the exchanging of a second set of wedding rings. There was not a dry eye amongst the bridal party, black love is beautiful. After being pronounced husband and wife again and sharing a kiss, Orchid placed a decorative broom at their feet before they jumped and made their way down the aisle.

The reception space had both Keon and Kiko speechless. Everything was perfect……even down to the area set up for pictures. It was more than Keon ever expected from Orchid and less than he thought it would cost. If she had to spend a million dollars on the wedding, it didn't matter to him. As long as he had his wife and child in his life….everything else would fall in place.

After introducing the bridal party and the couples' first dance, the wedding party, and parents that were present took pictures. Kiko insisted on a special set of pictures with just she and Orchid but let Keon jump in on a couple.

Guests mingled and enjoyed the open bar while dinner was being served and the pictures were finished, for the time being. It's normally the best man that makes the first toast, but Keon switched that up, not being able to hold his emotions inside. "What up ya'll?!" Keon yelled into the microphone. "Hey!" everyone answered in unison and applauded.

"I know I'm a lil outta line, but I need to say something. We need to give a special thanks to our sister, best friend, therapist and anything we ever need...Orchid. You are a dream come true. For those of you who don't know.....Orchid planned and executed this whole shit, 'cuse me, by herself, and kept it a secret from her nosey best friend." he said and laughed. "This is tight right?" he asked receiving applause. "You are a strong, beautiful black woman and we are so fortunate to have you in our life and for you and D, may he rest in peace, bringing us together. So.....as a small token of the love that we have for you, I got you a lil something. Aye Boz.....open it up!" he yelled.

Boz pulled the white drapes that covered the massive windows to reveal a black hard top convertible Benz, complete with rims.

"Thank you O.....we love you." he said putting her in a bear hug.

"No you didn't!" Orchid yelled.

"Yes I did."

"I need to get in on some of this love....and where is my Benz?" Kiko said and laughed.

"Since you must know....it's in the garage at home. What you know about that!?"

There were jokes, memories, and more jokes for the

next half hour while toasts were made during dinner. Afterward, it was time to take the kids up to Kiko's younger sister who was not quite old enough to party with the big dogs......and to change Kiko into her reception gown.

"Mom, I wanna party with you." D whined.

"You can't Doo. You and Keona are gonna have a ball with Tiara. I got you your favorite games, DVD's, finger paints, and a whole fridge full of all the snacks you and Keona wanna eat."

"I can really eat all I want and you won't get mad?" D asked smiling excitedly.

"You sure can and tomorrow, I'll take you and Keona to D & B for games."

"For real aunt Orchid?!"

"Yup, we'll go in the afternoon time okay. Now listen to Tiara, I'll be back to check on you." Orchid said kissing them both.

She went back to the room to check on Kiko and pull on the blunt she'd jacked from Keon earlier. She walked in and busted Kiko doing the give it up in the mirror.

"Drop it like it's hot!" she yelled walking in the door.

"Come here you." Kiko said opening her arms to hug her best friend. "I can never ask for or imagine a better friend, sister....than you. You have truly amazed me with your strength, love.....and all that other shit. I can never repay you for what you've done for me but what I will do is always promise to be the best friend and auntie I can be. I love you soooo much." Kiko said hugging her again.

"I love you too.....and all I want from you is your friendship......and maybe some free weed from time to time. " Orchid laughed. "You wanna hit this before we go down?"

"Hell yeah! Speaking of hitting it, Khalil looks like he's ready to rip that dress off you girl. And did you check the hounds all in his face?" Kiko laughed.

"Yeah, I noticed but he's single and can do him."

"Wh….this is me you're talking to. Come on……you feeling him aren't you?"

"To be honest…..it may be love."

"What! Did I hear the L word?"

"Yeah…..but I'm taking my time with it. To be honest Kiko, I doubted that I could love another man after D. You know when he died, it was like my heart had been ripped from my chest….and there was a fear that it may happen again with him being in the streets. But….I can't live in fear. Thanks to you and your husband staying on my ass, I'm at a place where I can love." she said wiping away happy tears. "But…..I won't say it first." she said and they laughed.

"Technically, you wouldn't have said it first. I mean to him yes but…..Khalil asked us about it."

"About what?" she said almost choking on the blunt smoke.

"He loves you. He just doesn't want to tell you and you push him away. He wants to make sure you're ready. So…..are you?"

"I'm as ready as I'll ever be…..I guess."

"You're ready…..and you know I'll be here every step of the way to help you through."

"I know ma….thank you. I love you."

"I love you too….you just make sure you're saying those words to Khalil sometime soon. Let's get back downstairs before your brother puts an APB out on me."

With no kids present and those who had a

problem with the way they partied gone, it was time to cut loose. Liquor was flowin, blunts were being blown like it was legal and the bumping and grinding on the dance floor popped off. When it was time to catch the bouquet, Orchid was ready to run but Shaunie ushered her back onto the floor.

"Aiight ladies…..you ready!?" Kiko yelled tossing the bouquet practically into Orchid's hands.

"Uh oh my dude!" Boz said laughing. "She gonna want something."

"Uh oh? See…..that's why she with me and not you, cause of thinking like that. Any man I know would kill for a wife like her."

"I thought ya'll were just…..kickin it. You wifed her?"

"Not officially but it's going down." he said already decided to tell Orchid how he felt about her later that night.

After the ladies cleared the floor and a couple shots, Keon walked over to Kiko and took her hand.

"Alright ma…..let me show them what a real pair of legs look like." he said guiding her to the chair and sitting her down. "Don't ya'll nigga be eyeballing my goods either." he said and laughing into the mic before going up her dress and pulling off her garter. "Aiight……who want this?!" he said and tossed it. Boz caught the garter and had a smile on his face. He was cool with Khalil on the strength of Keon, but he was definitely hating. The way he saw it, he was an outsider and Orchid needed to be with someone from her city….namely him.

"Aiight sis, come take the throne." Keon yelled.

"Wait….you took off the wrong garter boy. It's the one that was on the bottom. I keep this one." she marched over and snatched it from Boz. "See!" she said showing him the engraved charm that hung from it.

"Shit…..that almost got me killed. Aiight…..we gotta do this again."

"Thank the Lord. Boz is cool but I don't want his hands anywhere near my snatch." Orchid whispered to Shaunie causing her to crack up.

"Aiight…..this is the real deal." Keon said tossing it. "My nigga Lil!" Keon yelled when Khalil caught the garter. "Aiight, aiight…..let's do this. Come on sis."

All the fellas barked and hooted as Khalil keep inching her dress and the garter higher…..and higher. Being close enough to her now wet pussy, he had to swipe her clit and lick his finger afterward. She felt her face become hot and her pussy begin to juice just from the quick touch. He stood to his feet, took her from the chair, and kissed her. The DJ started spinning "Seems Like You're Ready" by R. Kelly and he pulled her close. Everyone on the dance floor was in the zone, feeling on their partners, ready to get it in.

For Khalil, the reception couldn't be over fast enough. He was glad when things wound down and the re-married couple was ready to head up to their suite. After all parties insisted, Keona and D stayed in the suite with Theresa. After meeting and falling in love with Khalil, she was determined to see him and Orchid together, especially after seeing the effect he had on her daughter. The old Orchid was back and better than ever. She wanted happiness for her daughter.

After checking on the kids and showering, Orchid made her way to Khalil's suite. The fellas wanted to have a night cap and a blunt so she left them to it. She was in the shower when he text her a picture of the hard dick he had waiting for her. She put her leggings and long tee over the nightie she had on and took the elevator up to his floor. As soon as she walked through the door he was on her. "Damn......been waiting all day to touch you like this. That dress had me stuck on hard every time I looked at you." he said running his fingers through her hair.

"Oh, so you were looking at me? I didn't know you did.....with all the groupies you had in your face." she said jokingly.

"Fuck them......it's you I love." he said looking into her eyes and pecking her lips.

"You what?" she asked surprised.

"Come sit down with me." he said walking to the couch and pulling her onto his lap. "We've been kickin' it for almost what...six months now. I know you wanted to take your time, but I can't help feeling the way I feel. I don't want to push you away and if you don't feel the same...."

"Khalil...."

"Let me finish. If you don't feel the same, I understand. I just want you to be clear about how I feel about you. I love you and I want to be with you and you only. So......what you wanna do with a nigga?"

"Khalil......."

"Be real ma....it's cool."

"If you'd shut up......I can tell you that I love you too."

"Huh?" he said expecting the total opposite.

"I love you too. I just needed to be sure before I said anything to you....but I do."

"So....does that mean you're officially wifey?" he said and smiled.

"Yes…..if you want me."

"If? You're all I want and need in my woman. How could I not? And when I say, I love you….I mean it. No bullshit, no drama, no games….it's me and you. And my man Lil D."

"So…..now that you have me, what will you do?" she said seductively.

"I can show you better than I can tell you."

When Orchid woke up the next morning she felt brand new. For a split second she thought the night before was a dream, but the man she loved coming into the bedroom with breakfast for her was the best reality check she could get.

"Morning beautiful." he said sitting the tray on the night stand and kissing her.

"Good morning. Thanks….it looks good."

"Not as good as you….even with morning breath and a lil crust."

"What?! I don't have any crust."

"Yeah….aiight. It's cool. You could have a booger hanging out your nose and I'd still love you."

"I like that way that sounds."

"Me too. So dig…..I want you to eat and get dressed we got a busy afternoon ahead of us."

"What do you have in mind?"

"New York for a lil shopping. Sex in Central Park…." he said and smiled.

"Nice try. I'd love to baby but I promised D and Keona I would take them to D & B's for behaving yesterday. Can I get a rain check?" she asked kissing his neck.

"I'll do you one better. If it's cool, I'll hang with ya'll and we can do a lil shopping around here."

"See….now that's why I love you……and the way you look in this towel."

"That's too bad…cause it's coming off."

"Good, I got something under these covers for you."

"That's what I'm talking about!"

Chapter 20

After a long day of fun and games with D and Keona, Orchid was spent. Keona begged repeatedly to sleep over so she allowed it. She'd also keep D occupied so she could get some rest. After setting the kids up at the table with their McDonalds, she thumbed through the mail. She received her monthly letter from her brother. She opened it and read it with tears in her eyes. Her brother was finally coming home. Although she knew he's probably written her mother, she called her up.

"Hey pumpkin! How are my two babies doing?"

"We're fine and you? You haven't thrown out a hip messing around with that man of yours have you?" Orchid laughed.

"I got this thank you. How was D & B?"

"The kids had a ball. I wish you could've stayed longer."

"Me too…but I had to get back to work."

"Yeah….I just opened my letter from Byron. I can't believe it."

"Yes…..my baby is finally coming home. We have to plan a party or something."

"Definitely. I miss him….and I still hate that he didn't let us come see him."

"He said it would make his time harder, which is understandable."

"Well, he has less than a month…..so maybe he wouldn't mind now."

"I don't know…..but you know I'll be in town a couple days before he gets out."

"It better be before then."

"Yes ma'am. I gotta run…give my babies kisses

from me."

"I will….love you."

"I love you too."

Needless to say, the next morning Orchid was walking through the visitors' gate where her brother was being housed. She was nervous, stomach was in knots. She hadn't laid eyes on her brother in twelve years. How would he look? Would he be upset because she came? Did he miss her? A million thoughts ran through her mind.

After being processed, she took a seat at a table and waited until she saw what she thought her brother would look like. She watched inmate after inmate come out and greeted their loved ones and still no sign of her brother. She overheard a conversation and looked in that direction.

"Yo, I though ya'll said I had a visit? I don't see anyone here I know." Byron said irritated…wanting a visit. His upcoming release had him full of nervous energy.

"There's only one person waiting for a visit and she is fine. Over there." the guard pointed.

"I don't know who……hold up." he said walking slowly towards Orchid. "Excuse me….."

"Now don't tell me you don't recognize your own little sister." she said and smiled with tears in her eyes.

"O?! Is that you?!" he asked not believing his eyes.

"The one and only." she said and stood.

"Oh my fucking God!" he yelled and picked her up in a hug. "Look at you girl! Wow….my baby sis!" he hugged her with wet eyes. "Let me look at you." he said twirling her around.

"Look at you! All buff and handsome." she said with a sigh. "It's been a long time B."

"Too long. I see your still hard headed…..but I'm glad you came."

"So am I. So…..you gonna be a free man soon huh?"

"Yeah. I'm so excited I can't sleep at night. A little nervous too. I know shit is hard out there for a nigga fresh out and I'm not trying to go back to the streets."

"You won't have to worry about that unless you choose to. You not wanting for a thing when you come home."

"Really? Who got it like that to be taking care of a grown ass man? Mommy got cake but I got expensive taste. Unless one of you won the lottery."

"Actually, I did…..when I met the most wonderful man I could dream of. Then I lost him."

"I'm sorry I wasn't there to help you through that. Mommy told me a lil something about it."

"It was a tough time but I got through it thanks to Kiko and my honorary brother…..D's best friend."

"How is Kiko? She still a chubby little shit head?" he asked and laughed.

"Oh no! Ms. Kiko is supermodel material. Married with a beautiful daughter. We live right up the block from each other in Welesly Estates."

"Welesly estates?! Ain't those them high priced ass mini mansions they put up a few years ago."

"Yeah….I guess you can say that." Orchid laughed.

"Ya'll rolling like that!?"

"Let's just say we're not wanting for anything."

"So…….I got a nephew huh?"

"Yes and he's a hot mess. Wise beyond his years. He reminds me of you when you were younger along with his father. He's doing good with everything that happened."

"Good. I knew D way back in the day…..he was good peoples."

"The best. I miss him but….we're good now. I'll be even better when you get home and we can have a big ass party."

"I can't wait. A brother don't have no parole or nothing, so I can get it in!"

"I heard that. You know me and mommy will hook it up."

"I can't wait to see her. I still can't believe you're here." he said and hugged her again. "I think about you all the time yo. Shit, I had to beat a nigga ass over your picture too up in here."

"What picture?"

"Mommy sent me one of your pictures; I guess it was senior pictures from high school. Some pervert ass dude in here wanted it to jack off to. I went the fuck off."

"Wow! I didn't know I was that sexy in high school." she laughed.

"Why not….you all grown and sexy now." he smiled lovingly at his sister.

"Yo B…..what it do playboy!?" a more muscular version of Lance Gross said walking past.

"I can't call it. That's your woman?" Byron asked.

"Nah….my sister. She bought my daughter up to see me. Who's this fine young lady….your woman?"

"Nah….this is my sister Orchid. Orchid….this is my right hand man Alex, Big A."

"Nice to meet you. I didn't know they had such handsome men in here…..besides my brother."

"Okay….yeah, I'm in here. Nice to meet you." he said and kissed her hand. "She fly at the mouth just like you dog."

"I know that." Byron said proudly.

"It's nice to finally meet you….he talks about you a lot. I'mma let you finish your visit. I got your brother for a few more to chill with."

"When do you get out….if you don't mind me asking?"

"A few more days."

"Make sure you keep in touch too yo. My peoples is throwing me a big party."

"I'm there my nig. Nice meeting you again Orchid."

"You too."

"Listen at you….flirting and stuff."

"It's innocent. Besides, I have a man that loves me back home."

"He better be good to you."

"He is….I think you'll get along with him just fine. He reminds me of you."

"Oh….then he good people."

They laughed and shared memories the rest of their visit until it was time for Orchid to go. When it was, they held each other a long time before either of them let go. Byron told his sister he loved her and walked her to the door. He was glad to see her and couldn't wait until he was on the outside to get reacquainted with his family.

The day Orchid and Theresa had been waiting for had finally arrived, they were picking Byron up and bringing him home later in the afternoon. Not wanting to have a large party his first day out, Orchid arranged a small gathering of his close friends and family at her home. She also went shopping and made sure he had the latest gear, a cell phone and some fresh Timbs. He had been calling the house on the regular since their visit. He'd had the opportunity to talk to and become acquainted with Lil D and Khalil over the phone.

D was already dressed and off to school, so Orchid took the opportunity to lounge around a little bit. Her mom was out at the mall and Lil was in the hood, so that left her alone. Too restless to just lay, she smoked an L, cleaned her room, and got dressed. By the time all that was accomplished Theresa was back from the store and standing in her bedroom rushing her.

"Geesh woman....I'm coming."

"I've waited twelve years to see my baby, you're not gonna make me wait any longer."

"Alright! Lead the way bossy."

There were waiting impatiently at the gate for signs of someone coming out. Orchid saw his beard and bald head and knew it was him bopping towards the gates.

"Mom....here he comes."

"That fat man is not my baby." she said and chuckled.

"Yes....that is." she said getting out the car as he approached the gate.

"Baby sis! Free at last!" he said hugging her before picking her up and twirling her around.

"Man....fresh air. When's mom getting in?" he asked unable to see through the tinted windows.

"Well......" she said and knocked on the door.

Theresa emerged from the truck with tears streaming down her cheeks and came around the car where he could see her.

"Mom." he said in almost a sigh before he hugged her tightly.

They all stood at the car shedding tears of joy.

Their family was reunited. A few minutes passed before they let each other go and spoke.

"You're more beautiful than I remember." he said wiping away her tears.

"And your more handsome and chunkier than I remember." she said and chuckled. "This is a wonderful day.....I got my baby back." she said hugging him again.

"Mom...I apologize again for......"

"No apologies. You made mistakes, you paid for them. The only thing to do now is not repeat them."

"You got that right. Let's get outta here....I've had more than enough of this place. Who's car?"

"Mine." Orchid said proud of her Aviator.

"Aiight sis. This is nice."

"Thanks. Once you get official, I'll get you a lil something to push."

"You got it like that?!"

"Who.....big willy over there? Please. Come on.....let's get you outta here."

The ride to Orchid's house was unbelievable. They shared memories a few laughs and even fewer tears. Byron couldn't believe how much things had changed since he'd been gone. When they rode past the projects, he was flooded with memories.

"Do Aunt Val and them still live there?" he asked of his favorite aunt.

"Her crazy ass aint going nowhere." Theresa laughed at her sister in law.

"I gots to see her."

"She'll be over later."

"Over where?"

"Well, we wanted to give you a little time to get adjusted, so we're not having the big party just yet. But, your sister hooked up a lil something at her house for later."

"That's wsup…..thanks baby girl."

"You're welcome. Ok….home sweet home."

"Who's home?" he said staring at the large estate.

"My home boy…..and you can stay as long as you like."

"Get the fuck outta here!" he yelled. "Sorry mom."

"Boy, you're grown."

"You really live here O…..and with how many people?"

"It's just me and Lil D. Mommy and Khalil are here a lot but it's just us two."

"You done come up. What do you do for a living?"

"Nothing!" she and Theresa said in unison.

"Although the circumstances were horrible, D left me pretty well off. The only thing he wanted for me to do is be a full time mom to D. After being hard headed and burning myself out, I finally decided to make good on that promise."

"Damn girl. So what do you do all day?"

"Mom stuff….clean, cook, volunteer, take an occasional break for a blunt. Boring house wife stuff for the most part."

"I wanna be like you when I grow up…..minus the woman part." B chuckled.

"You wanna sit in the car and talk about it or go inside. Your nephew should be home in a few."

When Lil D got home and met Byron, he immediately took a liking to him. They played video games and wrestled….two of D's favorite things to do. He scampered off to his room for his favorite shows, so Orchid got busy preparing for their guests to arrive. She and Theresa sat in her smoke room, laughing and sharing a blunt while B showered and changed.

"Damn! Mom....let me know you chief when you had a fit when I did it." he laughed.

"You were a minor and I'm grown." she laughed and passed Orchid the L.

"B....there's liquor under the cabinet if you want a drink. Help yourself."

"I don't mess with the alcohol like that, but I will hit that blunt." he said sitting between the two of them. "This shit here is the greatest. Chillin' with the two ladies in my life."

"Speaking of ladies....what happened to that gold digging tramp that claimed she loved you so? What's her name again?" Theresa asked.

"Ewwww.....Shaniqua!" Orchid laughed.

"Actually...she came to visit me not too long ago when she heard I was getting ready to come home. She has three kids now....one of which she's claiming to be mine."

"Are you serious?!" Theresa shrieked. "That's bullshit....and if that's the case; why not say something to one of us?"

"Your guess is as good as mine but I'm gonna check this shit out."

"You damn straight. I can't believe her ass." Theresa spat.

"Enough about that trick....when the party getting started? I need to see my folks."

"Everybody should be on the way."

"Cool."

"O......where you at beautiful?" Lil yelled when he walked in the house.

"Smoke room babe." she said getting up to greet him.

"Heyyyy ma!" he said kissing her. "These are for

you." he handed her roses. "I missed you today."

"I missed you too. Come on, I got someone I want you to meet." she said taking his hand and leading him back into the room.

"There's my boy! So, I heard you're in love." Theresa got up to hug Khalil.

"Yeah….definitely am. I'm a lucky man. I got some for you too." he said handing Theresa a smaller bouquet.

"We're both lucky men. You must be Khalil."

"Byron…..welcome home man." he gave B dap and a man hug.

"Thanks bruh. Shit, I feel like I know you already….all the chat on the phone."

"Yeah….it's nice to finally meet you in person. I see you hanging with the ladies. They share their blunt with you?"

"This lil ass piece your woman gave me." he said frowning his face at the fraction of an L.

"I got you. I'm gonna steal him for a minute. We'll be upstairs ma."

"Don't get him too high, he has to be sociable." Theresa laughed.

"I got you Ms. T."

Khalil led B to the bedroom and immediately handed him his own blunt filled with some cat piss weed and lit it for him. He pulled it in and choked off the strong weed smoke.

"Damn!" he said coughing. "This shit is some official."

"The best there is. So…….I know you feel like a new man huh?"

"Hell yeah. Twelve years……that was too long to be away from my girls. What really fucked me up was not being here for Orchid when she lost her husband."

"Yeah….that was sad. D was good peoples…..one of the most thorough niggas I knew."

"You knew D?"

"Yeah….my brother was his best friend. We had some business dealings….chilled when I was in town."

"Ok….where you from?"

"New York. We lived here back in the day when my moms' was married to Keon's dad. We grew up together. When my mom passed, I came back to be near some type of family. That's when I met the love of my life…..your sister."

"So you do love her?"

"Man……that woman is my everything. Her and lil man make my life even more worth living. Shit, I'm hoping one day she'll be my wife but I wanna take it slow……wait until she's ready."

"I feel you on that. Thanks for looking out for her though….she's my heart."

"I wouldn't have it any other way. I know we just meeting and all but know that your sister is in good hands. I know if there's any problems I gotta see you and Ms. T."

"Then we good."

"Speaking of good. I know we don't know each other like that but any of Orchids family….it's all love. So I want you to take this." he said handing him a wad of hundreds. "Just a lil something to lace your pockets with."

"Good looking….thanks yo." he said giving Lil dap.

"No problem. Looks like your family is here. We better go down."

"I can't wait to see them crazy asses."

It didn't take no time at all for their small gathering to turn into a small party. Once a family member told a friend that Byron was home they told another person, and then another and they all wanted to come over. It's a good thing whenever someone in the family cooked, they did it big.....so all were welcome. After making sure Keona and Lil D were sound asleep, Kiko and Orchid were really ready to cut up. Orchid grabbed her glass and proposed a toast to her brother.

"I'd like to make a toast....to my big brother. So much time has passed us by, but the love is still the same. I just wanna say welcome home and welcome back to family. We love you."

"Love you too sis." Byron said and hugged his sister. "Man! Ya'll are too much. I was telling my man's in the bing how we do it big. Wish that nigga was here but he got another couple to do."

"We'll send that nigga a postcard." Kiko said and laughed. "Spark this up!"

"Yo Keon, you're a lucky nigga. If I knew she was gonna turn out like this, I wouldn't have put gum in her hair and tortured her." Byron said laughing.

"Yeah, I am lucky. That's my baby."

"You try to put gum in my hair now and I'll whip your ass!' Kiko said and laughed. "Aiight, what we really need to do is pull out a deck of cards and let me and my girl over here whip some ass in spades."

"Whip who's ass!? You mean get that ass whipped!" Byron said and laughed almost choking. "Me and my brother in law against you two chumps. Keon, I hope you don't mind but I'm about to whip on you wife's ass something awful."

"Just save some for me....cause I got next."

They played cards, drank, and smoked until the sun was damn near coming up. Theresa tried to hold out as long as she could but passed out around one in the morning. As Khalil and Orchid were going into the bedroom, she was coming out.

"Are you two just going to bed?"

"Yeah, Ms. Theresa. This one has had enough." he said holding on to a tore up Orchid.

"Lord, I done told her about that cognac stuff. Ya'll get some rest, I got the kids. Where's Byron?"

"He's sleep in the guest room downstairs."

"Okay. Good night....I guess."

Chapter 21

Orchid woke up around two that afternoon, in the bed alone and thirsty as hell. She grabbed the room temperature bottle of water on her nightstand and drowned it. She rolled a blunt smoked half and went into the bathroom to get dressed and hopefully find the energy to keep up with the kids.

She was standing in the bathroom naked and rubbing down with lotion when Khalil came in and startled her. He didn't say anything at first, he just watched her rub down her beautiful body.

"Finally up huh? How you feeling?"

"I'm fine, a little tired but good. You trying to make it seem like I'm an amateur or something."

"Whatever you lush." he said and laughed at her. "You need some help with that lotion?"

"No….because I know it'll lead to something else."

"I know how to behave." he said taking her lotion and squeezing it into his hand before he began to massage it into her back and ass.

"I already did back there."

"You missed a spot." he said kissing on her neck and rubbing her ass.

"Come on Khalil, I just got out the shower and we have a house full of people."

"And they all in the dining room. Now….give daddy a kiss." he said turning her around and sitting her on the sink.

"Kiss, my ass." she said giving in.

He kissed her lips softly and played in her already wet pussy. "Looks like somebody was ready for me." He sucked on her nipples while she fumbled with his belt until she got it open and his pants were around his ankles. He entered her in one thrust and moaned at the feeling of entering her warm walls.

"I love this pussy." he moaned.

"Just….the pussy?"

"All of you ma. Work that." he moaned as she put her leg up and he pounded her walls.

She scooted towards the edge of the counter, wrapping her legs around his waist and began working the pussy.

"Oh God!" he moaned loudly. "Shit O…." he said between sucking on her nipples.

"Is this momma's dick?"

"Hell yes! Fuck…..work that….shit!"

"Shhhh! Someone will hear us."

"Fuck that….this shit…..is….fuck!….too good." he grabbed her ass wanting to crawl inside of her pussy.

She leaned back, and began working her hips until she heard her juices as he went in and out of her. She tightened her walls and picked up the pace until she felt his legs shaking and his dick swell inside of her.

"Khalil….pull out. You're not…..wearing….a condom." she managed to get out right before he came.

"Shit. My bad ma…it got on the carpet." he said laughing.

"It's okay; you'll get me a new one."

"I'll get you whatever you want girl." he kissed her.

"Now we both gotta get in the shower."

After another quickie in the shower and getting dressed, Orchid finally joined the rest of her family downstairs. She was too upset when she saw her mother's bags packed next to the door.

"Look who's up." Theresa said and giggled.

"Whatever. Where do you think you're going?"

"I have to leave today…..duty calls. I do want to know if D can come with me, I'll bring him back next week."

"Byron, you leaving too?"

"Yeah, gonna hang out with ma for a while. Do some catching up. Don't be like that. We'll be gone a week."

"And ya'll taking my baby! I'm gonna be bored as hell."

"Oh…..I can go?" D said walking into the family room.

"Yes….you can go."

"Thanks mom, you're the bomb."

"Where'd you get that from?" Orchid laughed.

"TV…..and you." he said grabbing his coloring book and leaving out just as quick.

"If he don't sound like you when you were little. That's what you get!" Byron said and laughed.

"I was a good child, thank you. Anyway, what time is you're flight? I need to pack for D."

"I already took care of it."

"You just knew you were taking him huh? Can you believe this babe?"

"Hey…..I'm not in this one at all. Matter of fact, B….you wanna go burn something downstairs?"

"You ain't gotta ask me twice." he got up and followed Khalil out the room.

'We ain't that bad." they said and unison and laughed.

"I knew you'd let me, that's all. So…..when you gonna give me another grandbaby?" Theresa asked and smiled.

"No time soon. You have a baby."

"No can do! Change of life is on its way and I'm

looking forward to it." Theresa laughed. "Just think about it. With D gone, you can relax, get some work done and put in some work. My grandson needs company and you and that Khalil would have beautiful kids."

"What about marriage first?"

"That would be great but as long as it's in the cards, I'm good."

"I'm really ready for you to go. You need a ride to the airport?"

"No smart ass, our car will be here in a half hour."

"Damn, and ya'll didn't think to wake me up so we can do lunch or something?"

"You needed some rest, in fact…..go back to bed. We'll have plenty of time for that when we get back. We still need to go find Byron a car and maybe a place to live depending on where he's going to stay."

"I guess I'll have to deal with it then." she pouted.

"Yup….pretty much."

She hugged all of her family like they were gonna be gone for a year instead of a week. After giving D his normal instruction, she handed her brother some money and hugged him before they left out the door. As soon as they left she became sad. She went back into the family room, lit the half of blunt in the ashtray, and put her feet up on the table.

"Awww….look at that face. What's wrong?"

"I miss them already."

"It's only a week ma." he said sitting next to her and pulling her close. "You need something to do. You still owe me that rain check for New York, you wanna roll out?"

"Well….I guess." she said trying to hide her smile.

"Please, you know you souped. Let's roll out now."

"I need to change."

"Why? You look good the way you are."

"We shopping in New York, I need to look the part."

"Aiight, I don't wanna hear shit about your feet hurting."

"Alright, let me get my purse and some dough…"

"Don't even play me like that. I love you, you're my woman….I got you." he kissed her and took her hand.

One of the things Orchid loved about Khalil is that he loved to shop almost as much as she did. He took her from Manhattan, to Soho and made a pit stop in Brooklyn to see his family. He was convinced that he'd found the one, so it was time for him to introduce her to his family…..not that she knew anything about it.

"Baby…where are we going?"

"We going to check my family out." he said and grinned knowing she was about to flip.

"Family! Khalil, I know you probably already had this planned! Why the hell didn't you let me change clothes?"

"Ma, they not gonna be worried about what you're wearing. They checking out you as a person….and believe me, you're beautiful inside and out."

"Awww….thank you babe." she said and kissed him. "Don't think you won't pay for this little stunt either." she said checking her face in the mirror. "Damn!"

Khalil sat back and just smiled as his aunts, nieces, and cousins fussed over Orchid. Just like he figured, they instantly loved her. Khalil's aunt Lynn spotted him sitting in the cut with a goofy smile on his face. She grabbed her drink and took a seat next to him.

"You're in love aren't you….real love?"

"How you know all that?" he said nudging his aunt Lynn who was more like a second mother to him.

"One, you wouldn't have brought her here for us to give the once over. And…..it's written all over that handsome face. If it's any consolation, she gets three thumbs up."

"That means a lot."

"You better hope your cousin don't come up and here and see her. She's just his type."

"Shit, he'll get hurt over that one right there." he chuckled.

"So…how long you in town for? We should go out to dinner….cause I ain't cooking tonight."

"We were just here for the afternoon. She may need to get back."

"Nonsense." she said and got up. "Orchid, since I can't get an answer from your man over there….when are you guys going back? I thought we could go out to dinner."

"We can stay if you want baby. I'm in no rush to get back to an empty house." she said causing him to smile.

That was one of the issues with him coming to visit, he never wanted to leave.

"Aiight, we'll chill then. We'll get a room and go back tomorrow."

"Ya'll might as well stay the weekend. You know tomorrow is my birthday party at the club. It's gonna be poppin' in there!" his cousin Alissa said dancing around. "Orchid, holla at your man. I want ya'll there."

"It's your call ma."

"I need to get a few personal items from the store but yeah, we can chill. You know I'm always up for a good party."

"Aiight, well let's gather up the crew and hit the town. We can get a room while we're out."

"Why get a room when I have all these rooms here." his aunt pretended to be offended.

"Auntie, no disrespect….but we gets it in." he said hugging Orchid from behind.

"Watch your mouth around your aunt boy." she said slapping his hand and blushing.

"Child, we have that type of relationship. Don't be embarrassed." she laughed at Orchid. "You need to bring her around more often.

Lil, Orchid and Alissa sat on the porch getting acquainted and passing a blunt while his aunt and nieces got ready for dinner. Alissa was mad cool, so Orchid almost instantly took a liking to her. Just as Lynn was coming out the house, cousin Keith came pulling into the driveway with one of his boys.

"Oh shit! Big time done came to town." he said with a smirk.

"Fuck your cousin, who is shorty sitting on the porch with Alissa? She bad as hell." his boy Lyfe exclaimed.

"I don't know but we'll find out won't we." he said getting out of the car. "Look with the New York air done blew in! What's buzzin' cousin?" Keith gave Khalil dap and pulled him into a hug.

"I can't call it. Wsup with you? I see you with the new whip."

"You know….trying to make it do what it do. Hey mom….big heads. Where ya'll off to?"

"We're going out to dinner. So if you came home

expecting a hot meal tonight…..you can forget about it."

"Shit…we'll roll too." he said eyeing Orchid.

"Ahem…since my family is so rude, I'll introduce myself. I'm the better looking cousin Keith. You are?" he said kissing her hand.

"My wifey. Orchid, this is my cousin Keith."

"Nice to meet you Keith." she said shaking his hand. "Babe, we taking the car?"

"Yeah, we can all get in the truck. Keith you gonna follow?"

"Yeah." he said feeling some type of way. He was hoping Orchid was one of Alissa's friends he could smash.

After dinner and drinks, they all went back to Aunt Lynn's to chill a lil bit longer before they went back to their room. Keith left out after a while, sick to his stomach at the affection Khalil and Orchid were showing each other. After all the kissing and touching, Khalil's dick was hard and he needed some release…..ASAP.

"Aiight, ya'll…..we gonna head out."

"Already?" Alissa whined.

"We'll be back in the morning for hopefully, some breakfast." he said and nudged his aunt.

"I guess I can do that for you. Gimme a kiss." she said embracing her nephew. "Aiight now, don't have me cook all that food and you don't show."

"We'll be here." Orchid said looking at him.

"I like her…..spicy."

After talking on the phone to D, her mom, and Byron for a while, Orchid was ready to strip outta her clothes. She got back into the living room and Khalil was rummaging through the bags.

"What you looking for?"

"I must've left the L's at my aunts. I'm gonna run to the store right quick. You need something?"

"Some munchies……and a Pepsi."

"I got you." he kissed her and left out.

She ran the Jacuzzi; pulled out the half of blunt she had in her purse, lit it and climbed in. The combination of weed and the jets causing the water the gently grazing her clitoris, had Orchid horny as hell. Before she knew it, she was touching herself until she released her juices into the soapy water. When Khalil text her to say he was pulling up, she got out of the tub, dried, applied lotion and threw on a robe.

By the time Khalil walked back into the room, she was setting in a chair, legs wide open, and gently touching her clit. He laid eyes on her and dropped the bags he was carrying. He walked towards her, grabbing a pillow from the sofa, threw it on the floor and dropped to his knees…burying his face in her wet pussy. He inserted two fingers inside of her and played with her g-spot as he lapped at her clit.

"Is this….daddy's pussy?" he asked between licks.

"Yes daddy…..yes!" she yelled rubbing her hand over his soft hair.

"Come for daddy ma." he said sucking on her clit until it began to swell and then stopped.

"Lil……"

"I got you ma. Go on in the bedroom, I'll be right there."

He took a quick shower and walked into the bedroom where she was laying, waiting for him. He dropped his towel and walked over to the bed, his dick pointing at her. He climbed back towards her pussy to put down some more of his head game and she stopped him.

"Come on ma." he almost begged, loving the taste of her pussy.

"Lay down." she said finally deciding to break him off.

"What?" he asked confused.

"Lay down." she said patting the bed.

Once he was laid down, she straddled his face with her back towards him. He began lapping at her pussy as she gyrated on his face. When she leaned forward and he felt her warm mouth on his dick, he almost lost it. She moved slowly, taking all of his ten inched into her mouth a little at a time before slowly deep throating him.

"Fuck!" he yelled loudly. "Damn......ma...ma!" he stuttered as she continued working his dick.

"Is this.....ma's dick?" she said sucking on it faster, massaging it as she did.

"Hell.....hell yes!" he moaned. "Damn O!" he yelled as she picked up the pace.

He inserted his fingers in her again and sucked on her clit feverishly which caused her to go ape shit on his dick as she was getting ready to come. She exploded and felt the juices he didn't catch, slide down her thigh. He still hadn't come, so she continued. Not able to take the tongue lashing she was giving him, he began eating her pussy again as a distraction.

"Ugh.....fuck ma!" he grunted as he was about to come. "Shit.......shit!" he said half yelling as he emptied his seeds into her mouth.

She slid down to his dick and inserted it inside her and began riding him slowly.

"Fuck! You's a beast tonight ma." he said holding

her waist as she moved.

"Shit!" she said and stopped moving.

"What? Why'd you stop?" he whined.

"You don't have a condom on."

"Ma….we don't have any. I wasn't expecting this."

"Well, I guess you've had enough." she said and went to move.

"Nah!" he said and held her in place. "Where you going?"

"To get in the shower. I told you….no glove, no love."

"Yeah." he said as he began moving and tapping her walls.

"Ka…..Khalil…..stop." she was barely able to moan.

"You telling daddy he can't have none of his pussy?" he said kissing her and still tapping her spot.

"Not…….without…a…..shit! Condom!" she moaned as he played with her clit while she started moving again.

"You know I love you and this is your dick. I got you…..I'll pull out."

"You better." she said and began bouncing on his dick.

"Fuck! Work that pussy ma." he moaned feeling his self about to come.

"Lil! Oh……shit!"

"I'm……getting ready to……come, ma."

"One minute……" she said feeling herself getting ready to come again.

He turned her over and long stroked the pussy from the back until she was calling his name and his dick was white with her juices. She began fuckin back at him at he came instantly, legs too week to move.

"Fuck! You know I got you right?"

"I know nigga. I'm not having any more kids right now, just so you know."

"What you saying, if you get pregnant you not gonna have my baby?"

"I'm not saying that. If it happens, it happens. I'm not trying to get pregnant on purpose though."

"I was about to say." he said pulling her close and playing with her nipple. "Yo! You gave me head." he exclaimed, after it popped back into his head.

"Yeah.....you like it?"

"You see you had me fucked up in the head. I love that shit.....and I love you."

"Well.....if you loved me, you'd fuck me....right now."

"We not fucking baby....but I will make that pussy do what it do."

Chapter 22

They ran a little bit late but they made it back to Khalil's aunt's house for breakfast. When they arrived, there was more family there than there was yesterday. Khalil welcomed the sight. He loved Jersey but New York and his family there would always have his heart. He actually thought about coming back but he hadn't planned on meeting and falling in love with Orchid.

"Man…..I see why you staying in Jersey, especially if the women look like this one you got here." his cousin Lonnie said eyeing Orchid.

Khalil chuckled at his cousin and Orchid's face when she made the comment. They always knew Lonnie was gay; it just took her longer than everyone else to figure it out.

"You know, dick is no good for you." she said and touched Orchid's leg.

"Uh….excuse me Lonnie." she said moving her hand. "No disrespect to you or your sexual preference but……I have to have dick. My doctor recommends a daily dose." she said licking her lips at Khalil.

"Well, when you change your mind…….holler at your girl." she said and winked.

"You need to chill with all of that Lon. That's not what up." Khalil said not finding the situation amusing.

"It's all good cousin. You got her."

After they cleaned up the breakfast dishes, Orchid left out with Khalil's cousin and niece's to do some shopping. They'd gone shopping the day they arrived, but she needed to get something club worthy. Just the shopping alone had Orchid contemplating her next trip and possibly relocation there. They hit the mall and didn't make it far before fella's were trying to holla. Most of them Alissa knew and were hyped about the party; others were trying to get in where they fit in. Orchid sat on a bench with her bags, enjoying her smoothie while Alissa got her mack on. One of the members of the all-male crew must not have gotten the hint when she walked away and approached her.

"Why you over here by yourself beautiful?" he said and took a seat next to her. "I'm Haneef and you are?"

"Orchid." she said and gave him a half smile.

"You gonna be at the party? Maybe we can get a drink and get to know each other a lil better."

"I don't think my man would like that very much and he'll be there."

"Oh.....you got a man huh? You love him?"

"Very much."

"Well, you tell him that I said he's a lucky man. If he mess up, holla at ya boy."

"I'll keep that in mind." she said and rolled her eyes as he walked away.

"Girl, these niggas is hounds. You ready to roll?"

"Yeah. I'm gonna need a nap before we go out. I had almost no sleep last night.

"If you and Lil stop freakin and take ya'll asses to bed, maybe you won't be tired." Alissa said and laughed.

"I might have to try that......later."

"I can't believe you going out on me like that!" Orchid said and pushed her brother. He decided he was going to live in Arizona with their mother. Being back on his old stomping grounds would possibly lead him back to the streets, so Arizona it was.

"Don't be like that Orchid. You know I'll be back to visit. Shit, as much as mom comes down here you probably won't have a chance to miss me." he said and hugged her.

"Whatever. I guess you're making the right decision."

"I know I am. I'm gonna miss you and my lil man's though."

"We'll miss you too. You trader."

Orchid got Lil D out of school early so they could all spend some time together before it was time for their flight. D had been buggin Byron about a video game he wanted, so they went to the mall to get it for him.

"Mom, you know what would be nice?"

"What's that D?"

"This gun to go with the game. Can I get it?"

"I don't know.....can you?"

"May I?"

"I guess so....but we gotta get two. I wanna play."

"Yeah! You're the best." D said and ran over to the counter where the guns were held."

"Yo, my nephew is so smart....and handsome. You doing a good job with him."

"Thank you. It wasn't easy at first. I was depressed and he looks so much like his father, it was a challenge. I knew I needed to step up to be mother and father and bam.....you get my sweet baby. Eight going on eighty six." she laughed.

"Yeah but he's not one of those grown ass annoying kids. I went by Shaniqua's crib and all her kids were wildin' out. She was just chillin' letting them fuck up. I can't stand that shit. If her daughter is mine, she coming with me."

"Are you serious?"

"Hell yeah. My seed ain't gonna be raised like that. We were disciplined and respectful. I mean, I made my mistakes but I never disrespected my family.....period."

"I feel you on that. Well, I guess I'll miss you."

"You guess? Whatever nigga."

The week had flown by before Orchid knew it. She could now get some much needed rest and relaxation and since D was going with his Grandma Debbie for the weekend, she could sleep as much as she wanted. Orchid decided to leave the office early, so she went to D's school to pick him up a lil early and take him to lunch.

"I'm so glad you came mom. The lunch is nasty.....unless they're having pizza, hamburgers or chicken nuggets. Why don't they have steak?"

"Steak is a little expensive, I guess they didn't have the money to buy enough for everyone." she said and laughed. "Is that what you want....a steak?"

"Yup. I want steak with skrimps at Applebee's."

"It's shrimp baby." she said and laughed. "Steak and shrimp it is."

"Am I still going to Grandma Debbie's today?"

"Yes, why?"

"I just wanted to know. I have fun with her and my cousins. She always shows me new pictures of daddy when I go too. I wish I knew him."

"I wish you did too. Just know that your daddy loved you so much. He couldn't wait for you to get here." she said getting a little sad at the memories.

"Are you sad? You miss daddy too?"

"I miss your dad every day and I'll always love him"

"I thought you loved Khalil?"

"I do but I loved your daddy first. We were married, created you, and loved each other a lot. We loved each other so much that I still love him."

"I get it."

"Do you really?" she answered with a smile.

"Yes. Just like I love my friends from our old house still, even though they're not here. Same thing almost…..right?"

"I guess you're right."

"I know about sex too!"

"What!?" she shrieked almost swerving. "Who told you…..never mind. This is too much for me." Orchid laughed. "Now I need a drink with my steak."

"Don't worry mom, if you need to know anything….I'll help."

"Ain't this a bitch?"

After D schooled her on sex over lunch, she was too through. She couldn't wait to tell Kiko about that conversation. After stopping off for a bottle of wine for Debbie, they headed to her house.

"Well if it isn't two of my favorite babies!" Debbie yelled and hugged them both.

"Hey grandma!" D hugged her. "Where's Tim and Keisha?"

"Upstairs….go on while I talk to your mother."

"Ok. Love you ma!" D said and kissed her. "Call me if you have any questions." he said and took off up the stairs.

"Questions about what? Come on here and sit chile."

"D seems to think he needs to teach me about sex."
"He what?!" Debbie laughed. "That boy is a mess. So, how you been doing?"
"I can't complain......I'm happy, D's happy. That's all I ever wanted."
"Glad to hear."
"How are you? You know we're still waiting for you to come to our house."
"D made me promise to come for Christmas, and I did. You mind if I bring his cousins?"
"Not at all. It'll keep him outta our hair."
They talked for a few more minutes before Orchid got up to leave.
"It's always a pleasure to visit with you mom. Oh, I almost forgot to give you this." she said handing her the wine.
"You must've known I'd need this with all these kids here. Thank you. Oh.....I almost forgot a package came here for you."
"Came here....why?"
"I don't know. It came addressed to you and Lil D." she said handing her the box.
"Thank you. I'll call later."
"Relax, you look tired. I got this."
"Oh.....okay then. I love you."
"Love you too....get some rest."

Not ready to go into the house just yet, Orchid stopped over to visit Kiko. She just had to share the conversation with her girl. Since Keona was out with her father they had some alone time to spark up and chit chat.
"I can't believe you're here on an unscheduled visit." Kiko laughed.
"Whatever bitch. You act like I don't come see my family. And I needed to see your face when I tell

you about the talk I had with your nephew." she said before she ran down all the pointers D gave her about sex.

Kiko fell out. "Girl, I need to get me a pen and paper to write some of that shit down. He is too funny!" Kiko said continuing to laugh.

"His grandma just did that same thing. Speaking of, let me open this box she just gave me. It came to her house for some reason."

"What's so damn funny up in here!" Keon said walking in with Keona on his back. "What up sis?" he said kissing her on the forehead. "Hey ma." he kissed Kiko.

"Auntie Orchid, where's D?" Keona asked.

"He's with his grandma this weekend but we're having you over the following weekend."

"Okay. Love you guys." she said and skipped off to the room.

"Let me hit that." Keon said taking the blunt from Kiko. "What brings you by unannounced?"

"Same thing I said." Kiko laughed.

"Fuck ya'll! I come visit."

"Sometimes. Let me call your man and tell him you're here…..since you been ignoring his calls."

"I have not. I was having quality time with my baby. Shit!" Orchid yelled.

"What's wrong?"

"Look at all this money." she said after opening the box and seeing the neatly wrapped bills.

"Where'd you get that from?" Keon asked becoming immediately suspicious.

"It was delivered to D's moms' house addressed to me and Lil D."

"It's something else in here." Kiko said reaching inside. "There's a note in here for you and Keon."

Orchid tore open the envelope and it read: "It's perfectly legal and for you and Lil Man. It's almost over…..you'll be safe and where you belong." she was confused.

As soon as Keon read his note, he jumped out his seat. "I gotta make a run, I'll be back."

"Keon….should I be worried?" Orchid asked a little scared.

"You good ma…….damn good."

"I wonder what that was all about." Kiko said.

"You and me both. So….since your man went on a top secret mission, ya'll wanna go shopping?"

"You don't have to ask me twice."

After a few hours and a few thousand spent shopping, Orchid dropped Kiko and Keona off before going home. She dropped her bags, showered, put on sweats before rolling an L, and curling up on the sofa. She was watching old Boston games when her cell rang.

"What….you don't love me anymore?" Khalil asked.

"Of course I do. I was having lunch with D and then talking with his grandmother. I just sat on my ass and blazed up ten minutes ago. Now……I can chill. I miss you."

"I miss you too ma. You feel like company?"

"When it's you…..always."

"I'll be there in ten."

"Use your key."

When Khalil walked into the living room, he was greeted by Orchid dropping her robe revealing her beautiful bronze body. He began coming out of his clothes as he approached her. His dick was at full attention when he reached her, so she took advantage of the situation climbing into his arms, wrapping her legs around his waist and inserted him into her wet pussy.

"Damn…..ma! I missed….you too." he said biting his lip in pleasure.

"Yeah…..show me." she said not missing a stroke as he fell onto the couch.

"Damn…….I should patent…..this pussy. Only for me……fuck!" he moaned. "Fuck this……my turn." he said placing her on her back and putting her legs over his shoulders. He pounded into her while playing with her clit, enjoying the rare privilege of feeling her insides without the interference of a condom. He fought hard to keep from coming, her yells and moans of pleasure pushing him closer to the edge. Not ready to come, he pulled out dove into her pussy face first. Orchid arched her back and began shaking and coming from the sensations shooting through her pussy and then the rest of the body.

She laid on the couch sweaty and limp after her orgasm. Khalil stroked his dick and licked her juices from his lips ready to put in some more work. He plunged into her as she flexed her walls, showing off her pussy control, until she'd milked him dry. She held him in her arms, as he laid on her chest….his limp organ still inside of her.

"I'm sorry ma…..I didn't make it out in time."

"It's cool. My ass went and got on the pill fuckin' with you and this dick." she said clinching her muscles around it, waking the sleeping giant.

"Aiight…..you gonna start something."

"Consider it started."

After a couple hours of love making, they showered and Orchid went downstairs to start on dinner for them. She'd barely heated the pan when came up behind her, kissing her neck.

"How am I supposed to cook with you all over me?"

"You're not supposed to cook. We need some quality time."

"We are having quality time."

"Away from home. Go get dressed, we have a plane to catch."

"Plane......to where!?"

"Vegas baby! Let's go!"

       While Khalil was breaking every traffic law to get to the airport in time, Orchid called to let Debbie, D, and Kiko know they'd be gone for the weekend in case they needed her. Orchid slept their whole flight, tired from her long day and their love making. Khalil gently shook her awoke when they were getting ready to land so she could see the lights of Vegas.

       As soon as they checked in, they changed, had a late dinner and hit the casino. Not really one for the tables, Orchid left Khalil and headed for the slot machines. All it took was a few minutes for her to catch slot fever. She ignored all phone calls and texts that didn't come from her family.

Getting tired of the slot machine taking her money, she got up and moved to a slot area that seemed more appealing. Just as she was getting ready to go in, Kiko called her phone.

"Hey Ms. Vegas. What ya'll doing?"

"Khalil's on the tables and I just sat down at another slot machine. What's up with ya'll....Keon get back?"

"Hell no! He called me and said he had some urgent

business to take care of out of town and he'd be back Sunday. You didn't read his letter?"

"No….I didn't open the box until I got to your house. Did he sound okay?"

"He sounded excited, but said there was nothing to worry about."

"As long as he's okay. Girl, let me call you when I get back to the room. This slot machine is going off and I don't know what's going on."

"Aiight, win some money for me. Love you."

"Love you too."

After claiming a small jackpot, Orchid set out to find a frustrated Khalil sitting at the crap tables. She crept up behind him and wrapped her arms around him.

"Why the long face babe?"

"These tables are kicking my ass. How about you?"

"Yoooo eleven!" the dealer yelled.

"Word! I finally win a hand when you come over. Let me know you're my lucky charm." he said and kissed her as he placed another bet.

"You ain't know."

"Hard six!" the dealer yelled.

"Oh….you might as well sit your fine ass down right here. I might just win some money with you by my side."

They played craps for the next couple of hours, winning Khalil's money back and then some. Tired of watching Khalil win all the money, Orchid got in on the game too. Khalil was wrapped up in the game and she'd had enough and was ready to smoke.

"Babe, I'm going back up to the room. I need a blunt and the bathroom."

"Come on ma, a lil bit longer."

"Call it quits while you're ahead. I'll be waiting."

Orchid had time to smoke a blunt, talk to Kiko for almost an hour, roll another blunt, and run the water in the Jacuzzi and still no sign of Khalil. She filled the oversized tub with bubbles and rose petals, stepped out of her clothes, and into the tub. She puts up her hair, lit the blunt, and sat back to enjoy. She was halfway through the blunt when she heard Khalil come in.

"Ma.......where you at?"

"In here?" she yelled. "How'd it go?"

"My winning streak turned into a skid mark after you left."

"Awww......daddy need comforting?" she said seductively.

"I'm always in need of that."

"Come on in here."

She admired his body as he took off the clothing he was wearing, licking her lips at the thought of feeling his manhood in her mouth. He stroked his hard dick and climbed in the tub behind her. He took her sponge and began squeezing the hot water over her breast as he kissed her neck.

"Have I told you how much I love you?"

"Not lately. I might need to hear it again."

"I love you ma. You make everything in my world alright. As long as I have you and Lil man in my life....I'm good."

"I love you too baby." she said leaning back and kissing him.

"I need to holla at you in the bedroom, you ready to get out?"

"I just got in. What's the rush?"

"I need to be inside of the woman I love right now. Turn around.......hop on."

She put the blunt in the ashtray and did as she was told. She parted his lips with her tongue, letting it dance with his as she slid down on his dick. She began moving slowly as he sucked her taut nipples. He reached his hand in the water, searching until her found her clit. He worked it with his thumb as she worked her hips, pushing him to the brink. She tightened her pussy on his dick as she slowly moved up and down, water splashing her hair as their skin slapped. Khalil held onto her waist as he thrust into her, tapping her walls until he emptied his juices inside of her.

"I love you ma." he said looking into her eyes.

"I love you too."

Orchid and Khalil couldn't stop smiling on the drive home from the airport. They hardly left the room the rest of the weekend. They spent the rest of the time catching up on sex and enjoying some quality time with each other. An added bonus for Khalil was that they weren't using condoms. He would love to have a child with Orchid but thanks to the pill she was taking, that wasn't gonna happen. In the meantime, practice makes perfect.

Chapter 23

The first stop back in town was to pick up D. He damn near jumped into Orchid's arms when she walked into Debbie's house, talking to her a mile a minute. She missed him horribly and listened to every word until she realized he wouldn't stop.

"D let me talk to Grand ma for a minute and we'll go. Go grab your stuff." she said and smiled at her son.

"So how was Vegas?"

"Great, I even won a little money. Let me ask you......have you received any packages or money?"

"I did receive a blank mother's day card this year and I have extra money in my account."

"That package you gave me had money in it. Will you let me know if you get anything else?"

"Actually, you got a letter." Debbie said handing it to her.

She opened the envelope and there was a note that simply said, "End it.....soon."

"What does it say?"

"This is strange." she said handing Debbie the note. "Let me know if you or I get anything else as soon as you get it."

"I will."

She stopped at McDonalds to get D something to eat and went over to Kiko's to meet back up with Khalil and let D and Keona play for a while. As soon as they walked through the door D took off running for Keona.

"Damn sis, what you been doing to my man? He come in here cheesing like he done won the lottery and shit."

"I did win the lottery nigga." Khalil said pulling Orchid close and kissing her.

"We both did." Orchid perked.

"You got that nigga pregnant, didn't you?" Keon said laughing. "Ya'll win some money?"

"Yeah, but you know how them tables be bruh."

"I know that shit."

"Next time….I go with you bitch." Kiko said pushing Orchid.

"Fine. Oh…I heard they have some wonderful strip clubs for the ladies there too." Orchid said with a smirk.

"I'mma kill one of them greasy ass niggas if I find any of them near my wife." Keon huffed.

"We ain't married, but that goes double for me. Fuck that, I got all the shit you need to see right here."

"Aiight, you doing too much nigga!" Keon laughed.

"Hater. O, you ready to roll?"

"If you'd round up D, we can go." she said and watched him leave the room. "So Keon…..did your impromptu trip have anything to do with that note and are we in danger?"

"It had everything to do with the note. No you're not in danger and no, I'm not telling you what it said. I was making good on an old promise and that's all you need to know."

"There was a letter at Debbie's when I got back there. All it said was "End it soon." This shit is strange."

"Whatever you do don't panic. You're good."

"You know more than what you're saying but I'm gonna let it go for right now." Kiko eyed him.

"Whatever."

"Aiight ya'll. Kiko….call you later ma."

        Although he can definitely be a handful, Orchid was happy D was on his Christmas break from school. They'd be able to spend quality time, play video games, and he'd taken quite a liking to shopping. His first morning home, he came stumbling into her bedroom with breakfast on a tray.

"Awww! My baby is so sweet." Orchid beamed.

"I'm not a baby but yes, I am sweet." he said and cracked a smile. "I guess for you, I'll be your baby."

"Why thank you. Did you do this yourself?"

"Yup. Waffles, syrup, and O.J."

"Thank you D."

"You're welcome mom. Are we still going shopping?"

"Yes, but you know we're shopping for other people's gift right?"

"Yeah, but there's nothing wrong with getting myself something. Can I get the Xbox with the connect thing? It's on sale at Target and I have enough for it."

"Let me guess….Uncle Keon gave you money."

"He always gives me money. I just save it in my bank."

"How much money do you have?"

"Last time I counted, I had twenty Benjamins. It might be more now."

"Wow….okay. I guess you can get it. You go get dressed while I eat this beautiful breakfast and get dressed. I have the doctors' first than we can go shopping."

"Are you sick?"

"No…..just a regular checkup."

"Okay, I can deal with that." he said walking out the door. "Love you mom!" he yelled back.

"Love you too!"

Feelings of joy, fear, excitement, and sadness overcame Orchid as she walked to her car. Joy and excitement the strongest two…..but she just couldn't help thinking about her first pregnancy and how happy she and D were. She hoped to have as much of a pleasant experience with Khalil as she did with D.

"Is everything okay mom?" D asked with his eyes still locked on his PSP.

"Everything is perfect. Can I ask you a question?"

"Sure….you need more sex help? And when can I have a little brother or sister? You love Khalil right?"

"Wow, one question at a time……and no, I don't need your sex help. Yes, I love Khalil. How do you feel about him?"

"I love Khalil. Him and Uncle K are like two more dads. So, what's up with a sibling?"

"Boy…..who have you been talking to?" Orchid laughed.

"Your baby is smart, right?"

"You sure are. Well, it's funny you ask about a brother or sister. My doctor just told me that I'm having a baby."

"Really mom!?"

"Yeah. It seems he or she will be born in seven and a half months. You okay with that?"

"I'm more than okay….that's great. Can I call Keona and tell her?"

"You can tell her later, I wanted to tell you first….then Khalil."

"Ok....but hurry, this is exciting."

Every store they went into and walked past the infants section, D just had to look. He already wanted to buy things for the baby. She was happy that he was just as happy, if not more than she was. D was giving her his version on babies, when Khalil called.

"What it do ma?"

"Oh it's doing alright. I'm out shopping with D, picking up some Christmas gifts."

"Oh Mom, is that Khalil? Did you tell him.....can I tell him?" he perked.

"Tell me what?"

"We'll talk later. Am I seeing you tonight?"

"Of course."

"Mom.....tell him."

"D....keep it up and there'll be no Xbox."

"Oh....tell Khalil I said wsup." he said bowing in defeat.

"Must be something big, wsup ma?"

"Khalil, I'd like to have this conversation face to face. So, please just wait until later."

"Aiight. So, where ya'll at?"

"We just got to Target. He wants to get his game system and I need to grab a few things. We should be home in a couple of hours."

"Aiight, I'mma let you get to it. I'll see you in a lil bit. Love you ma."

"Love you too." she said and hung up.

They were in the electronics section picking out some games to go with D's game system they were purchasing when Khalil strolled up holding a bouquet of flowers. He put his finger to his lips to silence D who'd seen him first and snuck up behind her, kissing her neck.

"Boy…..you were about to get pepper sprayed." Orchid said clutching her chest. "What are you doing here?"

"Came to check on the people I love."

"Nigga please. You brought your ass out here because someone was raising hell about me telling you something. But guess what….this still is not the place."

"Orchid…..stop playing with me and spill it." he said both worried and a lil scared.

"Please mom." D begged through clinched lips.

"How do you feel about children?" she asked Khalil knowing she had no choice.

"I love 'em. If it wasn't for them damn pills you poppin, I'd already succeeded in getting you pregnant."

"Well, apparently those pills weren't shit because here I am……a month and a half pregnant with your child." she said and smiled.

"See that's……what did you say?"

"I'm pregnant. Found out earlier today."

She watched for his reaction, but he turned his back. Khalil was so happy tears escaped from his eyes, which he was trying to hide. Fuck it, it doesn't matter, he reasoned and the excitement really set in.

"Yeah! Them birth control pills and no match for what I'm packing! Yes…..yes! I love you girl!" he picked her up and kissed her. "Yes! We having a baby!" Khalil was yelling loud as hell.

"Yeah! Can I tell Keona now?! You happy Khalil…..I am?"

"I'm more than happy Lil man. We need to celebrate! Let's finish this up and go out to dinner. When we get back home, we gonna have a private celebration." he whispered to Orchid and kissed her.

"See…..that's what got me pregnant now."

"Fuckin' right!"

Khalil ran a couple errands to give Orchid and D some alone time, which gave him time to put a few things and place. He also wanted to call his Aunt Lynn and tell her the good news. Khalil was happy beyond words. He'd always wanted children, but wouldn't dare impregnate some of the bitches he'd dealt with in the past. He lucked up and got the whole package when he found Orchid.

"Hey! Is everything okay?" his aunt answered the phone.

"Everything is fine; I just called to check on my favorite auntie."

"Boy please. Yeah you probably called to check on me but I can hear it in your voice you got something to say. So spill it."

"You know me too well."

"Damn right! Now stop stallin'"

"Aiight, aiight. I'm gonna be a father…..Orchid's pregnant." he said and smiled.

"That is wonderful news! Congratulations! How far along is she?"

"A month and a half. We found out today. That woman is giving me everything I've ever wanted."

"I can tell. Well, since you've found the one, you know what you need to do…..right?"

"I know Auntie….but she's been married before and buried her husband. I don't know how she'd feel about it."

"The only way to find out is to ask. How long ago did her husband pass?"

"Six or seven years ago."

"If she feels the same way about you, she'll say yes.

The fact that she's having a child, starting a new family with you is evidence of that. Just talk to her…..and I better see ya'll before New Years'."

"I'll bring her up this weekend. We should have some free time."

"Alright, keep me posted."

"I will, I gotta run auntie. I love you."

"Love you too."

"Wsup K?" Khalil answered.

"Who told you that you could impregnate my sister nigga?" Keon yelled through the phone.

"I didn't know I had to ask nigga. What up dawg?"

"Chillin'….yo, congratulations. You finally getting that seed you wanted."

"Yeah, I'm happy as hell. I'm out here checking on shit and picking her up a lil something before I go back over."

"That's wsup. D's excited."

"Too excited, he ratted her out."

"Word!" Keon laughed. "That's my nephew boy. Aiight, holla at me in the a.m. I know once you under Orchid's ass it's a wrap for the night."

"True dat nigga. I holla."

By the time he got back to Orchid's she was showered, changed and had the bed looking like Santa's workshop. He admired his beauty before he went over to the bed and kissed her.

"What was that for and why the goofy look? You high?" she laughed.

"High off you. Do you know how happy you make me?" he said kissing her neck.

"Very."

"As long I have you, D and now this baby……everything else doesn't matter. I know the circumstances were unfortunate but I thank God for you girl."

"Aww babe. I'm thankful for you too. I'm gonna whip your ass if your child messes up my shape, but other than that......I love to pieces."

"Damn! How you gonna threaten your future baby daddy?"

"Very easily."

"Can I ask you something?"

"Of course." she answered while clearing the bed, wanting some dick.

"You ever thought about getting married again?"

"Of course. Marriage was a beautiful experience for me. It's becoming a widow I can do without. I decided a long time ago, before I met you that my life had to keep on going. No, I'm not spending forever with D.....but I still want that, every woman does. Why do you......Khalil? You wanna get married?"

"The thought has definitely crossed my mind. I could see myself sitting on a porch, smoking a blunt with you....gray hair and all. The thought has been on my mind even more so today. I got something for you."

"Khalil.....are you serious?!" she asked when she saw the pink diamond ring.

"Ma, this.....is not an engagement ring, it's a promise ring. I promise to make you my wife whenever you're ready to take that step. Whatever you need, I'll wait for you. I would love nothing more than for you to be my wife......but in your own time. And when you do......I have that engagement ring for you too." he said sliding the ring on her finger and kissing her.

"When I do say I'm ready do I get to keep this ring too?"

"You can have whatever you like." he sang mimicking T.I.

"Then give it here." she said and smiled.

"What?" he asked confused.

"The engagement ring....but after you ask me properly." she said with glassy eyes.

"Are you.......hold on." he jumped up and went in his coat pocket. He knelt in front of her and took her hand. "Orchid, the day I met you, my world became complete. I love you....and I love D....and the baby you're carrying. Let me be the one you wake up to every morning for the rest of your life.....your husband. Orchid.....will you marry me?"

"As long as I get to smoke a blunt......yes, I will marry you." she said with tears tickling her cheek.

"I guess I can let this one slide."

"Then I'll be you're wife."

"I was already the happiest man alive....what's above that?"

"The happiest man alive with a wife." Orchid laughed.

"Fuckin' right! I love you Orchid."

"I love you too Lil!"

Chapter 24

Bright and early Christmas morning D was barging into the bedroom waking Orchid up. He scared the shit outta her jumping on the bed and she was ready to snap.

"Boy! You scared the shit outta me." she fumed but began laughing when she saw she scared him a little. "I'm sorry baby. I thought it was an earthquake or something. Come here." she said and pulled him into her arms. "Merry Christmas my love."

"Merry Christmas mom. I'm sorry I scared you."

"It's okay. So, I guess you're hungry....or do you wanna open gifts first?"

"We can eat 'cause you have to feed the baby. I saw on TV that you can't have coffee, it's bad for the baby, so I hid it from you."

"Uh....gee thanks. I can have one cup."

"I knew you'd say that. So grandma is downstairs making some."

"She's here already?"

"Yup and she's mad at you."

"Why?"

"I thought you told her I was having a little brother or sister and I said something. I'm sorry."

"It's okay. I tried to tell her but she's been busy. I'll be right down."

"Oh, Uncle Byron said to brush your teeth first. Oh and he brought my new cousin Lissette. He said she was lost for a while but he just found her. She's cool too."

"I sure missed a lot this morning." she mumbled to herself.

Orchid took a quick shower and was

standing in front of the sink rubbing down when she felt a thick dick slid between her legs and enter her slowly. She moaned in ecstasy as he plunged into her wetness. She turned around and sat on top the counter to allow deeper access.

"Merry......fuck.....Christmas ma." Khalil said between strokes.

"You too baby. Now....shut up and keep fucking me."

After a quickie and cleaning up, they joined the rest of her family in the kitchen. Her mom had already had breakfast prepared and sitting on the table when she arrived downstairs. After Theresa chewed her a new asshole, they got caught up and Byron filled her in on the beautiful little girl sitting at the table with them. Come to find out, Shaniqua's daughter was Byron's. Her trifling ass was more than willing to give up custody and Byron happily accepted. She was excited about getting to know her new niece.

After everyone's bellies were full, it was time to open gifts. It's a good thing Orchid is a shopaholic and can't turn down a good deal, so she had some jewelry that was fitting for a twelve year old girl. She didn't want her to feel left out and also planned on taking her to do a little shopping.

D was beyond happy with his barrage of gifts. There were clothes, IPod, video games, jewels... all kinds of unnecessary shit under the tree for D. Khalil went above and beyond for him. He gifted him a pair of custom Jordan's, a small Armani wardrobe, and the gift that made all of them go crazy for different reasons, an ATV.

"Mom, can I ride it....please!?"

"You don't know nothing about that thing and neither do I."

"O….if you don't mind, I can give him some pointers. It's modified with a speed limit; I even brought the helmet and all that protective shit." Khalil said.

"Come on O….he's a boy. What you gonna do…pamper him all his life, have him doing ballet?" Byron laughed.

"Don't get slapped Byron." Orchid warned.

"Fine…..but after we clean up and you get dressed. You can do it for a lil while, then we gotta go see Grandma Debbie and Keona."

"Okay mom. Thanks." D hugged her.

"Not so fast lil man. I have a couple gifts for mommy."

"Khalil, you just gave me two…….."

"Hush all that. Let's do this one first." he handed her the large box.

Orchid pulled out a chinchilla jacket with matching hat and hand warmers.

"Oh my God! Lil……this is hot! Thank you baby." Orchid said and kissed him.

"You're welcome ma. Take this one next."

She had a puzzled look on her face when she pulled out the helmet with her name airbrushed on it.

"I know. Now this gift, you can't have full access to until after the baby. Merry Christmas ma!" he said turning on her garage light to reveal the T-rex he gotten her. She'd talked about a bike but wasn't confident in her skills. "So, now you'll have three wheels instead of two."

"Thank you. I'm gonna ride it."

"O…..what did I just say?"

"I'm not showing yet. I'll let you come with me." she said and bat her eyes at him.

"Aiight…..just for a lil bit."

"Damn nigga…..let me know she got you pussy whipped like that." Byron laughed.

"Hey, it is what it is bruh."

"Shut up Byron and take notes. Maybe you can get and keep a woman." Theresa said and laughed as she left the room.

After they'd finished with breakfast, they made stops at Debbie's, Kiko and Keon's and even Orchid's Aunt Val's. They saved Kiko and Keon for last knowing they would be there for a while. Orchid also needed to talk to Keon. She'd received another letter with just a date for the following year and a simple sentence, "Talk to Keon." So, that was what she was gonna do. After they exchanged gifts and pleasantries, Orchid pulled Keon to the side.

"So, what am I supposed to talk to you about and what the fuck is going on?" Orchid asked tired of bullshit answers.

"Look, D has a very powerful relative with a complicated legal situation. He's knows you're family now, so he wants to take care of ya'll."

"Well who is it and am I in danger?"

"You're fine girl. Now you know if anything is going down concerning you and my nephew I'm on it. Am I right?"

"Yeah….you're right?" Orchid mumbled.

"Aiight then. He can't contact you directly and I can't say anything more than what I'm saying now. Sometime next year it'll be okay for you to meet. Until then, leave the shit alone. I got you."

"You wouldn't lie to me K would you?"

"You know we better than that. Now, let's talk about this niece you're carrying. Cause Keona needs a girl to play with. I love my baby but I ain't too beat to sit in them tiny ass chairs sipping tea…..and neither is D. That's why they beefing now." Keon said cracking up.

"They are too much."

"Yeah, gotta love them. Look, I gotta skate for a couple to handle something for the peoples. Keep your girl company and when I get back, don't make me have to drug test you. I know ya'll asses."

"We good. You just make sure you're careful."

"Always sis….always."

*****

A few days later in a remote location.

"She having a baby by this motherfucker!? What the fuck?! I gotta do something."

"It's already done dawg. She waited almost seven fuckin' years before she even attempted to date another man. She did what she had to do to hold it down for Lil man and her. She was fucked up man. Not saying it's gonna be easy, but Lil is good peoples, that's the only reason I even let shit go down. Just think about it D." Keon said passing D a blunt.

"I guess you right. I just wish I could hear her voice….touch her…..taste my pussy."

"Aww….come on man."

"And my man's! He just like his daddy, I can't wait to chill with him."

"Yo, he is something else. He's smart as hell, vocabulary off the hook. And that lil nigga will hold on to a dollar. I love him, that's my dawg."

"Good looking out for him K…..for both of them. I love you for that."

"That's family….and I know you'd do the same for

me. Yo........it's hard to believe I'm sitting here talking to your ass. It's like some crazy ass dream and shit."

"Yeah, I know. I was not having leaving my babies behind but you know not to fuck with the powers that be. I can't wait 'til I get back though. Shit gonna be real bad for that nigga Preme. They on him hard, so when I knew he was the problem.....it made missing my family a little easier to deal with. I just gotta digest this whole pregnancy thing."

"The answers will come my son."

"You still got jokes. I missed you my nigga."

"I missed you too D. Oh, check your girl out on Christmas."

"Look at her fine ass. Tha nigga Khalil better enjoy the good life now, cause when daddy's home.....it's a wrap."

"That shit is gonna be hella interesting....but we'll deal with that when the time comes. Ten more months yo."

"I'm counting nigga."

Back at the ranch....

Khalil and Orchid had just finished making love repeatedly and laid wrapped in each other's sweaty bodies. They were happy and Orchid felt safe in his arms....in his world. Just the thought of being his wife made her giddy.

"What are you smiling about?"

"Thinking about soon being your baby mama....and wife. I'm happy."

"That's all I wanna do......make you happy."

"You know what would make me happy right now......a soda and some leftovers. We're hungry."

"Listen at you. You go hop in the shower, I got you."

Just as Keon requested, he was getting a new niece, who was refusing to leave Orchid's body. She was three days overdue, July was the hottest month of the year and it was an everyday struggle for her not to be miserable. Khalil had been great, waiting on her hand and foot when he could. When he came home one afternoon and found her chugging mineral oil to go into labor, he rarely left her side.

They were laying on the couch watching one of Orchid's favorite movies, when the baby decided she wanted to get active. It felt like she stepped on her bladder so Orchid got up to relieve herself.

"Where you going ma?"

"Your daughter is tap dancing on my bl.......ahhhhhh!"

"What's wrong?!" Khalil hopped up yelling.

"My water just broke." she said smiling through the pain. "Finally."

"Okay....okay, what should I do?"

"Call the doctor and get my bag outta the closet. I'm going to shower."

"O....you in labor and you wanna take a shower? Come on ma."

"I'm not going to the hospital wet. It'll take me a minute." she said disappearing into the downstairs bathroom while Khalil scattered.

By the time she got out the shower, her contractions were kicking her ass.

"Khalil!.....get over here!" she yelled in pain.

"I'm here ...wsup?"

"We gotta go. This little girl is whipping my ass."

Kaliah Janay Wakefield came into the world raising hell July 26th, weighing in at 7lbs 8 oz at 10:33pm. Khalil was almost moved to tears when he laid eyes on his precious little girl for the first time. She had his nose and dimples but the rest was all Orchid. He left out of the room so they could clean her and the baby up, but he returned to their side right after.

"I have never seen anything more beautiful….well, besides you ma." Khalil said and kissed Orchid.

"Yeah….we did make a beautiful baby. I'm glad she's outta my body because she was three times as bad as D. She made me think twice about having any more kids."

"Unh uh ma…..we got two, three more to go." Khalil said seriously.

"Did they give you some drugs too?"

"Hey mom!" D came charging into the room with balloons and a teddy bear.

"Hey big man!" she said hugging her first born.

"Ya'll got here quick."

"Not quick enough for grandma. She fussed the whole way here."

"I see he's in here snitching on me." Theresa walked in on his report. "So, how are you feeling and where is my granddaughter?"

"She's already running the nurses. She'll be back soon."

Before hospital staff knew what hit them, Orchid's room was filled with her family. They were only supposed to be two at a time but Keon shut that down as soon as the nurse stepped into the room. Kaliah was passed around so much her parents hadn't had twenty full minutes alone with her. Theresa noticed them having a moment on the bed with the baby and D, so she immediately started cleaning house.

"Alright, I think that's enough for one day. Let's let them have some alone time with the kids."

Orchid was thankful her mom was such a take charge woman, because she didn't want to kick out the people who loved and cared for her most.

"I'll be outside waiting for D. We'll be back in the morning. I love you sweetie."

"I love you too mom…..thanks."

"I thought they'd never leave." D said causing Khalil and Orchid to laugh. "She's so tiny….and pretty."

"Yeah…but before you know it you'll be wishing she was a baby all over again. She's gonna grow fast just like you did. I want you to remember that you will always be my baby and I love you and Kaliah the same."

"Oh, I know that mom. And I'm gonna be the best big brother ever to you." D said kissing the baby's hands. "You know you have to wait six weeks before having sex again…..right Khalil?"

"Wow!" Khalil fell out laughing. "Thanks for letting me know lil man. You got all the answers huh?"

"Not all……most of them though. I told mommy, that's how she got pregnant."

"Okay Mr. Wizard, that's enough sex education for you. Give me a kiss, so you and grandma can get to whatever it is she has planned for you."

"Ok." he sighed. "I love you mom." he said and kissed her lips.

"I love you too D….always."

"I love you too Khalil…but you don't get a kiss. It's not manly."

"I love you too Lil man." he laughed and gave him

a pound.

The birth of Kaliah brought Orchid's family unit even closer together. So much so that it was becoming a problem for Lil that he had to come over every day to visit like he was just a baby daddy and not a husband to be. Khalil and Orchid were laying on the bed cuddling, since that's all they could do, and he brought up the subject that had been on his mind.

"I wish it could be like this every night....you waiting for me in our bed when I come home."

"It's pretty much like that now babe."

"I mean in a home we share. I want you and the kids with me."

"Babe, your place is nice but it's not enough room for all of us."

"We don't have to stay there ma. We can live where ever you want."

"Khalil....I'd love to be with you all the time. Let me have a talk with D about it and I'll give you an answer."

"Don't keep me waiting ma, this is important to me."

"I got you daddy." she said and kissed him.

"How much longer we got before I can get in my pussy?"

"We have the doctors on Friday.....two more days babe. Until then....I think I can hook you up with a lil education."

"That's what I'm talking about."

After the doctors Orchid decided to pick D up from school early to spend a little time with him before taking him to the airport to meet her mother.

Since Kaliah was knocked out in her car seat, she took the opportunity over lunch to bring up moving. "So D….how are things with you and Khalil?"

"Mom, you know me and Khalil are tighter than tight."

"Okay…" she said and laughed. "Well, how would you feel about living with Khalil?"

"In his house? It's nice but it's smaller than our house."

"We wouldn't live there. Khalil said that you and I can pick out whatever house we want to live in."

"For real?!" D perked. "Do I have to leave my school?"

"No, not if you don't want to. Actually I wanted to stay close to your aunt and uncle."

"I say let's go shopping for a new house then! You're not gonna start without me while I'm gone are you?"

"Not at all. I'll wait until you get back to start looking."

"Alright!" he perked. "I love you mom."

"I love you too D…..Always will."

Chapter 25

Since D was leaving for the weekend and they'd just gotten the green light for sex, Khalil wanted some uninterrupted quality time. He booked a suite, made dinner reservations, and asked Kiko to keep the baby for the night. He packed up the baby and told Orchid to be ready by the time he got back. She showered and put on a tunic, tights and her boots and was ready when he pulled into the driveway.

"You are too fine to be waiting for me on the porch." Khalil said coming up the porch steps and kissing her.

"You seem more than ready to roll, so I figured I'd meet you halfway."

"See, that's why I'm making you my wife. Let's roll ma."

They did dinner, drinks and dancing on the ocean at the Continental and hit the casino for a while. After all, they were in Atlantic City. Seeing Orchid bending over the crap table, her ass looking perfect, he was ready to go up to the room. He left Orchid at a slot machine while he went upstairs to run the Jacuzzi. He filled it when her favorite mango bath bubbles and threw rose petals in the water. He called Orchid to come up, rolled a couple blunts and popped the bottles. She walked through the door and a smile spread across her face.

"Look at you....trying to seduce somebody. Don't worry, I was giving up the pussy anyway." she said and smiled.

"You crazy as hell......and fine. Come here girl." he said and laughed, pulling her into his arms and kissing her. "Having my seed done made you thicker in all the right places girl." he palmed her ass.

"Yeah….I noticed. I look like a video hoe." she said and laughed. "So, do I get to drink first or we getting in the Jacuzzi now?"

"Come on ma; let me fill your cup."

They laughed, talked and made out like teenagers on the couch. It was the most fun Orchid's had in a while. She loved Kaliah, but she was hell while in the womb. Khalil felt bad at times for her, which was part of the reason he had to get her a banging push present.

"Ma….do you know how happy you make me?"

"You show me every day baby."

"Well, I got something to show you some more. It's a little something to show my appreciation." he said handing her a velvet box.

"Khalil!" she gasped as she looked at the flawless pink diamond bracelet. "This is……beautiful. Thank you."

"I figured you needed something to go with your necklace. I know I can never replace D but now you can have a reminder of both your great loves with you all the time."

"This means a lot Khalil. I love you." she said kissing him with tear filled eyes.

"I love you too ma. I hope those are happy tears." he said wiping a tear from her cheek with his thumb.

"Nothing but. Well, I guess now is a time to give you a gift. I talked with D…..and he's excited. He wants to look for a house as soon as he gets back." she chuckled.

"Word! We moving in?"

"Yes we are. You ready for this?"

"I been ready."

Needless to say the time they spent in the Jacuzzi was very short lived. Orchid ordered him to the bed while she changed into the skimpy lingerie and stilettos she just purchased and walked into the bedroom. Khalil took one look at the outfit and his dick turned the towel into a tent.

"Aw shit! Come her girl."

"Not so fast….I got something else for you. Bam!" she yelled tossing two boxes of magnums onto the bed.

'What's this for?"

"There will be no more unprotected sex…..for the time being."

"Come on ma!" Khalil whined. "We engaged and you on the pill."

"I have to be taking them for a month for them to be effective and I'm extra fertile."

"We were having sex for a minute before you got pregnant. Come on ma, I'll pull out."

"I got pregnant because it hadn't been a month. I don't regret it because I have my princess."

"Aiight then, we don't need those."

"Sorry baby….no glove no love."

"That's the bullshit O."

"I'll tell you what, you get your oral and five minutes unprotected as long as you don't go premie on me.'" she said and cracked up.

"Oh, you got jokes."

"Awww babe, it's not like that. Look, when we get it in, we get it in and I want to enjoy it without having to keep telling you to pull out. I wanna enjoy all of my dick without distractions."

"How can I be mad when you put it like that?" he said and kissed her.

"Aiight then." she said mounting his chest with her pussy staring at him through the crotch less thongs. "So....you've wined me, dined me.....now it's time to sixty nine me."

The sun was up when they finally tapped out. Orchid had more orgasms than she could count and all Khalil could do was lie there with a smile on his face. He had his future wife, his seed and a step son.....life was good.

It didn't take any time at all for Orchid and D to find the house of their dreams. They immediately fell in love with the same house.....for different reasons of course. They decided on a six bedroom, seven bath estate...complete with pool house, in ground pool, barbecue and all the modern amenities they could ask for and then some. Khalil was more than happy to put up the cash for whatever it was they wanted, as long as he had his family with him.

By November, they were packing up and moving into their new digs. Leaving all the furniture behind, Orchid and D only packed their clothing, toys and items they couldn't live without. All the furnishings in the house were brand new.....signifying their new beginning. Since Khalil refused to let Orchid contribute to the house, she purchased all the furniture before he had a chance to protest, had the house decorated and ready for them to move in in time for the holidays.

Orchid didn't see D for two days after they got settled in. Khalil insisted that he had a flat screen mounted in his room....one for watching television and the other for video games. He put a mini-fridge in his room, pinball machine, and any game D could think of he already had. Orchid had to force both of them at times out of the room to eat dinner at the table. Life was sweet......for the time being.

Summer time had finally rolled around and Orchid was gassed. She finally had a chance to utilize her beautiful back yard. What better way to christen it than with a BBQ. Not one to get dirty over a grill, she hired a cook, and bartender and was ready for a day of relaxation.

She was in the mirror admiring her new curves in her bikini and applying sun tan lotion when Khalil walked in and began eyeing her. She tried to ignore his stares, knowing they'd end up fucking but the tension was too much. He walked over to her without a word, closing the door behind him, and untied the sides of her bottoms. The skimpy cloth dropped to the floor and so did he. He placed her leg over his shoulder and began lapping at her clit. Within minutes, she was shaking and coming on his face and he was licking his lips. "Climb on ma." he said lifting her and leaning her back against the wall. "Fuck! I love my pussy." he moaned as he thrust into her.

She began working her pussy causing him to moan loudly. He picked up the pace and began tapping her walls as he sucked on her taut nipples. Feeling her legs shaking and slipping from his waist, he guided her to the bed and laid her down. He put on a magnum knowing he was getting ready to go hard and was not trying to pull out. He thrust in and out slowly, while he played with her clit and watched his dick go in and out of her wetness until the condom was covered in her juices. After making sure she was thoroughly satisfied, he began thrusting faster until he exploded with a grunt, falling on top of her.

"Damn girl! This pussy is my kryptonite." he said and laughed.

"Well now that you've gotten it all dirty, you gotta clean it."

"Oh, I can do that."

Ending up fucking in the shower, D had to play temporary host until Khalil came downstairs first to take the reign. "My dawg!" Khalil said and gave him pound when he took over. Keon, Kiko and Keon had already arrived so he darted out back in his trunks to jump in the pool with his cousin.

"Ahem!" Kiko cleared her throat. "How the hell ya'll invite folks over for a BBQ and ya'll upstairs fucking?"

"Nah....I was helping her with her suit."

"Un huh. Oh I heard...damn ma, I love this pussy!" Kiko quoted and laughed.

"What can I say, your girl got that.....I don't know what it is but I'm addicted."

"I see." Kiko laughed.

"You see what?" Orchid asked walking into the kitchen.

"That he's addicted to your pussy. What were you doing to him in there?"

"If I tell you, I gotta kill you." Orchid said and laughed. "Babe, I'm gonna get a drink and Kaliah is sleep. Will you listen for the monitor?"

"I got you."

The backyard was filled with their friends and family. There was a table for spades, dominoes, and chess. The kids were having fun in the pool on the slide Khalil had installed for D and the adults were drinking and flirting. The day had turned out better than expected.

"Um excuse me….where is my brother?" Orchid asked Kiko.

"He was acting strange earlier. He got a call, told me he'd meet us here and left out."

"His ass better get here before I'm too drunk to play spades. Shit!"

"What's wrong?"

"I think I should've sat out that last blunt."

"Why?"

"I think I just saw someone wearing D's chain."

"Lil D?"

"No…..his fathers."

She shook the thought and went back to their game. They had just dismissed a couple of Khalil's boys who thought they had game and was sitting back counting their money when Keon walked up.

"Ya'll not right….out here taking niggas money." Keon laughed. "You know I get a cut."

"You gonna get cut."

"It's about time you got here, your wife was about to call cheaters." Orchid said and laughed.

"What?! Stopping playing with me Kiko, you know I love you and we way better than that."

"Better be."

"Look, I need to holla at you a minute. You can have her back in a few."

Keon took her hand and led her into the house without so much as a word. It was killing her, so the silence ended.

"What is going on Keon?"

"I have something I need you to see." he said pulling her into the living room.

"What the……this is a real sick joke Keon."

"It's no joke Ko. It's me."

"How the…..when……"

"First time I've seen her speechless." Keon laughed and received a punch. "Damn, my bad."

"Damn, can I get a hug? Shit, it's been what eight, nine years."

"My bad….I'm just in shock. What happened?"

"We have plenty of time to get caught up on the technicalities. So, I have a niece huh? Ya'll look good."

"Yeah….you too. She's out there playing with……D." Kiko said her mind trying to register what she was seeing.

"I can't wait to see him. How's your girl?"

"She's great….with her ghetto booty."

"She grew a donk?" He laughed.

"Did she."

"Can you….get her for me?"

"I'll be right back."

Kiko stopped at the bar to order herself a refill and get Orchid a drink as well, she was gonna need it. She got back to the table and Orchid had their next opponents sitting at the table, talking them out their money.

"Hey, you ready?"

"I need you in the house for a minute. Oh and this is for you." she said Orchid's drink down.

"Everything okay?"

"Yeah. Bring that drink with you….you'll need it." Kiko held on to her hand tightly as they went through the house and to the living room. Kiko took a deep breath and opened up the sliding doors before they went in.

"What it do Ko?"

"Hey ma….long time no see."

"What the……" was all Orchid could get out before she hit the floor.

True Glory Publications

IF YOU WOULD LIKE TO BE A PART OF OUR TEAM,
PLEASE SEND YOUR SUBMISSIONS BY EMAIL TO
TRUEGLORYPUBLICATIONS@GMAIL.COM. PLEASE
INCLUDE A BRIEF BIO, A SYNOPSIS OF THE BOOK, AND THE
FIRST THREE CHAPTERS. SUBMIT USING MICROSOFT WORD
WITH FONT IN 11 TIMES NEW ROMAN.

Check out these other great books from True Glory Publications

She Used To Be The Sweetest Girl

Mancell's Reign: Daughter Of A Kingpin

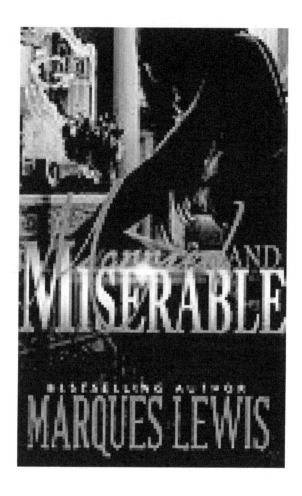